The Girl in the Mirror

Horla's Visit

JAMES WALKER

ILLUSTRATIONS BY MIKE BASTIN

Matador
9 Priory Business Park,
Wistow Road, Kibworth Beauchamp,
Leicestershire. LE8 0RX
Tel: 0116 279 2299
Email: books@troubador.co.uk
Web: www.troubador.co.uk/matador
Twitter: @matadorbooks

ISBN 978 1800460 751

British Library Cataloguing in Publication Data.
A catalogue record for this book is available from the British Library.

Printed and bound by CPI Group (UK) Ltd, Croydon, CR0 4YY
Typeset in 12pt Aldine401 BT by Troubador Publishing Ltd, Leicester, UK

Matador is an imprint of Troubador Publishing Ltd

In memory of Miss Moneypenny

Thank you, Margaret *(she went to Belvedere you know!),* for your encouragement, perseverance and painstaking eye for detail in the writing of this book.

Thank you also, Louie and Kenny for your encouraging reviews at the start of this journey.

For Lucy, Eleanor and Emily…my inspiration

Contents

1

THE GHOST
IN THE ROOM

'You know, Lu, it's going to be *so* different you not being around,' Eleanor sighed as she moved a piece on the chess board.

'Hmm, well that's not exactly true, is it, Elle?' Lucy answered, trying her very best to be brave.

'What do you mean?'

'Well *I* will be around; remember, it's *you* who's moving house today, not me.'

'Yes, I know… but you know what I mean – I'm *really* going to miss you.'

Lucy's stomach churned on hearing her best friend say that. She turned away as her eyes started to mist up, looking instead at Princesses Elsa and

Anna, gazing down at her from her bedroom wall. 'And I'm *really* going to miss you too, Elle,' she whispered softly in reply.

'But you will be coming to visit me, won't you?' Eleanor pleaded.

'Well, I'll try, but Dad says Liverpool's a long way away.'

'Oh, but it's brilliant. There are *so* many great things to see there.'

'I know, you've told me loads of times.'

'If you come, we could go to the World Museum Liverpool,' Eleanor then said, enthusiastically, 'it's got a dinosaur exhibition, a bug house with bugs bigger than my hand, and an aquarium with the most colourful fish you'll ever see.'

'Yes I know, you've told me that too,' Lucy added wistfully.

'And we could go to Knowsley Safari Park where there are *loads* of wild animals, including Amur tigers, and there are only *500* of them left in the whole world!'

'How do you know? Have you counted them?' Lucy asked, trying to sound cheerful.

'Very funny, Lu, but honest, you'd love it. Last time I went to Liverpool I visited Speke Hall. It's an ancient house and it's haunted by the ghost of a maid who dropped her baby down a thunder-box toilet.'

'Dropped her baby down a thunder-box toilet! You never told me about that.'

'Are you sure?'

'Yes, of course I'm sure – I'd have remembered that bit about a thunder-box toilet; *what the flippin' heck is that?*'

'It's a toilet they used in the olden days; it's made out of wood, and if you sat on it and trumped, it sounded just like thunder.'

'Ha ha, now that *would* be worth seeing.'

'Yes, and if you came, you could sit on it while no one's looking and try out the sound effects.'

'Cheeky, you know I don't do trumps.'

'Are you sure, Lu?'

'Of course I don't.'

'Neither do I,' Eleanor lied back.

At that very instant, the loudest fart they had ever heard in their lives echoed around the room. *Praaaarrrwwwwpppp*, it went, and stunned the girls into silence. For a few seconds they sat open-mouthed and wide-eyed, and then burst into laughter.

'Oh smacky-bumbums, Elle,' Lucy said, 'that was loud, my dad would have been proud of that. I wouldn't have thought you were capable of it!'

'Oh, Lu, you cheeky thing, you know very well that wasn't me.'

'Liar, liar, yer knickers are on fire!'

'But it wasn't!'

'It was you!' exclaimed Lucy and, picking up a pillow, she bashed her friend over the head with it.

'No it wasn't! It was you,' Eleanor squealed back in delight, picking up a second pillow to fight back.

'It *was* you.' – *Bash!*

'No it *wasn't*.' – *Bash!*

'It *must* have been you, because it *wasn't* me.' – *Bash!*

'It *wasn't* me either.' – *Bash!*

'Who was it then?' – *Bash!*

'Maybe the Speke Hall ghost has followed me here and she did it.' – *Bash!*

'If she did, then where is she now then?' – *Bash!*

'I don't know, maybe she's under your bed.' – *Bash!*

'Oh no, I've got to sleep here tonight with a ghost under my bed!' Lucy cried out, pretending to be frightened… before bashing her friend with a pillow once more.

And so the pillow fight went on until, near to exhaustion, they heard footsteps coming up the stairs. Eleanor whispered, *'It's the ghost!'* and they shrieked in pretend terror as the door opened – and in walked Lucy's mum carrying a tray with milk and chocolate biscuits on it.

'Hello. You two seem to be having a good time,' she said, 'I thought chess was a serious game.'

'It is, Mum, but Elle's just trumped,' Lucy giggled.

'I did not!' Eleanor protested.

'She did, Mum, and it was even louder than Dad's.'

'Stop exaggerating and have your refreshments.'

'Mmm, thanks, Mum, we need a break; we haven't completed the game yet and it's wearing our brains out.'

'Why is it taking so long?'

'Because we've been doing what Polo says we should do when playing chess: "Concentrate, concentrate, concentrate".'

'Well I'm sure he didn't mean you had to concentrate for three times as long. And you know, I don't think you should be referring to Mr. Jackson-Phillips as "Polo".'

'But, Mum, everyone calls him that.'

'That doesn't mean *you* have to!'

'His head does look like a polo-mint though, Mum.'

'Maybe it does, but I still think you should use his correct name.'

'But it's easier to call him "Polo".'

'Don't be lazy.'

'We're not being lazy, are we, Elle – we think it suits him, don't we?'

'Don't be dragging Eleanor into it – you were the one who called him Polo. Oh, and I've also heard about pupils singing "Powwwwwllo, Powwwwwllo" behind his back when he's on yard duty; you two don't do that, do you?'

'*No,*' both girls protested, shaking their heads innocently, even though they did.

'How did you find out about that anyway?' Eleanor asked.

'I heard about it on the mums' WhatsApp group; there's very little that happens that doesn't get mentioned on there. If Mr. Jackson-Phillips finds out you're referring to him, you'll be in trouble, big trouble.'

'Yes but…'

'Yes but nothing! Anyway, changing the subject, Eleanor's mum is due in an hour, so have your snacks, then tidy up this room – anyone would think you didn't have a wardrobe, Lucy.'

'But what about finishing our game?'

'Well, if you tidy this room properly – and why a game of chess should involve every other game you own coming out of your box is beyond me – you can use my laptop next week and finish it on Skype, how about that?'

'Oh that'll be great, Mum, thanks.'

'If your mum thinks this room is untidy, she should have seen mine yesterday,' Eleanor said as Lucy's mum disappeared downstairs.

'Why, what happened?'

'Well, Mum and I had just put the last of my things from the wardrobe neatly into one of the packing cases the removal men had brought, but before we had put the lid on it the men started to move the wardrobe—'

'Don't tell me they dropped it?'

'No, as they tipped it on its side to get it through the door, the most enormous spider dropped off, landed in the packing case and then disappeared amongst my clothes.'

'*Oh no!* Did you have to take the clothes out again to get it?'

'Well, my clothes did come back out again, but not nearly as neatly as they went in.'

'How do you mean?'

'Well, poor Mum, who as you know suffers from that arachna something or other and is unbelievably scared of spiders, screamed, tipped the case upside down and started kicking at my clothes; by the time she'd stopped kicking they were everywhere. Goodness knows what the removal men thought.'

'Ha ha, that must have been so funny.'

'Not for Mum it wasn't.'

'And did you find the spider?'

'No, we didn't, but Dad said he did. He came running upstairs to see what all the noise was about, then sorted everything out while I took Mum downstairs and made her a cup of tea to calm her nerves.'

'And what did he do with it?'

'He said he threw it out of the window, but it wouldn't surprise me if he hadn't because he likes to play tricks like that.'

'Oh crumbs, you could be sitting with your new

classmates next week when the spider suddenly appears out of one of your pockets!'

'Yes, that's what I'm afraid of. It's hardly the way to win new friends is it?'

'Oh I don't know. You could tell them it's your pet. "Meet Ida the spider", you could say; they'd gather round thinking you were cool.'

'Run a mile thinking I was weird, more like.'

'It'd get you noticed though.'

'Oh yes, it'd get me noticed all right. "Eleanor the Peculiar" they'd call me, *or worse.*'

Lucy joked and said, 'You *are* a bit peculiar actually.'

'Ooh, thanks for the compliment, Lu.'

'You're welcome, Elle.'

'Talking of pets, is that Pip I can hear outside?'

'No, it won't be; my grandma's not coming today.'

'I'll have a look out of the window just in case; it would be nice to see him one last time before I go.'

'Look if you want, Elle, but it won't be him.'

'Ah ah,' Eleanor said as she got to the window, 'no wonder it sounded like Pip.'

'Huh?'

'It's a Jack Russell like him, and its running round in circles chasing its tail. Come and have a look, Lu.'

'Flippin' heck, Elle,' Lucy said as she joined her, 'that dog's moving faster than a Catherine wheel at a fireworks display. The speed it's going it'll disappear up its own bum.'

'Oh, that is so funny.'

'It'd be funnier if it caught it though.'

'Nah, it'll never do it.'

'I think it will; it's getting closer.'

Suddenly, the dog yelped in pain as it bit its tail. The girls giggled as it stopped and looked around for whatever had attacked it while it was chasing the hairy snake that followed it everywhere.

'Have you ever seen Pip do that?' Eleanor asked.

'No, you'd never get Pip doing that sort of thing!'

'Too intelligent to waste his time I suppose.'

'No, too bone idle to waste his energy!'

Eleanor smiled and said, 'You know, I'm going to miss him; it was always nice to visit your grandma's and play with him.'

'And he'll miss you too, Elle; he always liked you making a fuss of him.'

'Well when Brenner died it was good to have another dog nearby to make a fuss of.'

'I thought you'd have another one by now.'

'Hmm, I think we just might be getting one when we settle in our new house.'

'Oh that's great.'

'And the reason I think that is because all of Brenner's things have been packed and are coming with us.'

'Ooh, that sounds promising – let's hope you're right.'

'Yes, so do I.'

The girls turned away from the window and had barely taken two steps when they stopped in their tracks and laughed.

Sitting on one chair was Ollie, Lucy's giant bear, and sitting on the other was Fred, her giant panda, both of whom had moved from their usual positions at the end of Lucy's bed where they usually stood like guards on sentry duty.

'Oh you are definitely good, Elle. Have you joined the Magic Circle or something? I mean, how *did* you put Ollie and Fred there without me noticing?'

Eleanor giggled and said, 'Oh, here we go again. You know very well it wasn't me. The question is, how did *you* put them there without *me* noticing?'

'*I* didn't put them there and *you* know I didn't put them there.'

'Ah, but as it wasn't *me*, it's obvious *you* did put them there.'

'Oh stop messing around.'

'*I'm* not messing around; it's *you* that's messing around.'

Lucy paused for a moment – she usually knew when Eleanor was pretending, but this time she was being serious, *really serious.*

'But it wasn't me, Elle, honest! I followed you to the window remember, so it certainly wasn't me who moved them.'

Eleanor looked at Lucy wide-eyed. She realised that she, too, was telling the truth.

'Well if you didn't move them, and I didn't move them, *then who did?*' she gasped.

The hairs on the back of Lucy's neck stood up and a tingle shot down her spine.

'*Aaaarrrrgh!*' she screamed, which prompted Eleanor to scream an even louder, '*Aaaarrrrgh!*' and, grabbing each other's hand, they ran out the door and down the stairs as quickly as their legs could carry them.

'*Mum, Mum, there's a ghost in my bedroom!*' Lucy shrieked as they burst into the kitchen.

Her mum turned and looked at them, peered over the edge of her glasses, and said, 'Have you tidied your room?'

'No, but, Mum, you don't understand, *there really is a ghost in my room.*'

'Is there really?'

'Yes, we went to look out of the window and when we came back Ollie and Fred were sitting on our chairs.'

'Oh they were, were they?'

'*Yes, honest!*'

'And neither of you put them there?'

'No. And also, Mum, I don't think it *was* Eleanor who trumped before.'

'No, it wasn't me, I told you it wasn't me,' Eleanor chipped in.

'Hang on. What you girls are telling me is that there is a trumping ghost upstairs in Lucy's *very untidy* bedroom.'

'*Yes!*' the girls said together, then giggled as they realised how ridiculous that sounded.

'Well of all the excuses for not tidying a room,' Lucy's mum muttered, walking to the broom cupboard. Reaching in, she pulled out a large feather duster with a one metre handle and, with a grin on her face, turned and charged at the girls shouting: 'Get up those stairs now and tidy that room... and get the ghost to help you... with three of you on the job it should be done in no time at all!'

The girls, shrieking in delight, ran out of the kitchen and up the stairs, feeling far braver than when they had come down.

'How ridiculous of me to think there was a ghost in my room,' Lucy said as she entered.

'Yes, but it's good to know that if we were ever in peril, from a ghost or anything, your mum will come rushing to our rescue with a grin on her face waving a flippin' big feather duster!'

'Ha ha, not sure she would scare anyone away though.'

'She scared us away!'

'Yes, back to my bedroom where you played the trick on me.'

'Oh don't start that again. You moved Ollie and Fred, and that's that. There's only so long you can keep a joke going for you know!'

'OK... keep your hair on, bossy boots. I won't mention it again... although how you did it I'll never know!'

'*Lucy!*'

'OK, OK... be modest if you like.'

'I am not being modest at all. You know very well I'm not... grrrrr.'

'Alright, calm down, calm down. That's settled then, you're not being modest. Now let's get these games put away before that scary woman with the feather duster comes back to tell us off again!'

2

ELEANOR LEAVES FOR LIVERPOOL

As the time for Eleanor to leave grew nearer, the girls sat on Ollie and Fred and talked across the table.

'You might as well know, there's going to be an almighty racket any minute,' Eleanor said.

'What do you mean?'

'Well I meant to tell you earlier, Mum's changed her car, and it's *sooooo* embarrassing.'

'How can a car be embarrassing?'

'Oh they can be, trust me, embarrassing with a capital M.'

'Don't you mean with a capital E?'

'Whatever.'

'What sort of car is it anyway?'

'It's a Volkswagen Beetle and she bought it second-hand from a lady who was a hippy in the nineteen sixties – well that's what Dad reckons she was.'

'A Volkswagen Beetle – they're my favourite car. I've never seen one that's embarrassing though.'

'You haven't seen this one!'

'What's embarrassing about it?'

'Well for a start, the exhaust has got a hole in it.'

'That can be fixed surely?'

'Yes it can, but I haven't finished yet.'

'Oh, go on.'

'It's pink.'

'Brilliant – there's nothing wrong with that.'

'And it's got flowers painted on the bonnet, the doors and the roof.'

'Fantastic, it sounds really good; I just can't wait to see it.'

'It's got eye-lashes, including one that moves up and down above the headlights to give the impression it's winking.'

'Oh, this gets even better!'

'And she calls it Betty!'

'Whoa, I didn't realise your mum was so cool.'

'Neither did I, and neither did Dad – he can't believe she's bought it and has refused to go in it.'

'Spoil his macho image eh?'

'That's what Mum says, although I must admit, at nearly two metres tall with a big bushy beard, he would look a little out of place in it.'

No sooner had Eleanor said that, than a sound was heard in the distance. It was a banging sound, and it got louder… and… louder… and louder.

'That sounds like Betty,' Eleanor said as the noise stopped and a car door slammed. 'It looks like I'd better be going.'

Lucy shot to the window and, looking out, said, 'Wow that is one fantastic looking car!'

'Pity it doesn't sound fantastic.'

'Oh I don't know, I think the noise adds to its image. It's sort of saying, "Look at me, I'm different".'

'Oh it's different all right – very different. You haven't got a balaclava I could borrow have you!?'

'Ha ha, you're so funny,' Lucy said, reaching out for Eleanor's hands, realising again how much she was going to miss her. 'Are you excited, about moving I mean?' she asked.

'Yes, I'm kinda like dizzy with excitement – Nanny and Grandad are too: they're going to take me for days out during the school holidays.'

'Oh, you mean, "yummy, but don't tell Mummy" days.'

'That's right, loads of sweets and chocolate and crisps and ice-creams and stuff; I can't wait!'

'They're my favourite days too; sometimes I struggle to eat my dinner after being out with Grandma.'

Eleanor smiled and said, 'Sometimes I think my mum suspects.'

'Yes, I think mine does too because she gives me a suspicious look, then I force it down and she's happy.'

'That's exactly what I do.'

'Once, when I was about three, Grandma slipped up. She knew she wasn't supposed to give me chocolate but we were in a café miles away, and she bought me a rice cake covered in chocolate—'

'Oh, I love those,' Eleanor said, licking her lips.

'—yes, so do I. Anyway, after finishing it, I had chocolate all around my mouth, which Grandma thought so funny, she took a photograph.'

'Oh no, that's evidence, you don't want your parents seeing that!'

'Well, ahem… when we got back home Grandma realised she'd left the camera in the café.'

'Oh flippin' heck – what happened then?'

'Mum phoned the café and it was still there.'

'*Phew* – that was lucky, it could have been stolen!'

'Yes, but then Dad picked it up on his way home, and after dinner they looked at the photos and saw my mouth covered in chocolate.'

'Uh oh, what happened then?' Eleanor asked.

'Dad laughed his head off, while Mum just looked at me over the rim of her glasses; I think she was trying not to laugh, but I'm not sure.'

'I don't suppose it mattered then because they were just your milk teeth.'

'Well it seems to matter now because Mum makes me brush my teeth for twice as long after being out with Grandma. "It's alright for Grandma because her teeth are like stars, they come out at night", she nags.'

'That's true; I saw them in a glass of water when I went to her house for a sleep-over with you, do you remember?'

'Yes I do. Apparently, Grandad Freddie, when he was alive, said that Grandma did so much talking during the day that her teeth carried on talking even after she'd dropped them in the glass of water at night.'

'He sounds a funny man – just like my grandad.'

'Bet you can't wait to get to Liverpool to see him.'

'I can't, and Nanny too of course. Oh it's going to be so good there, and it'll be even better when you come and visit me!'

'I'm really looking forward to that Elle, in fact you've talked about it so often that I'm almost as excited as you are. Now promise you'll get in touch next week and tell me all about your new school, and what you get up to with your new friends.'

'I promise Lu, and you promise to persuade your parents to come and visit us as soon as possible.'

'I will, I promise, because I'm so looking forward to visiting those places you've talked about.'

'And I can't wait to show you them, because I know we'll have a great time.'

'Brilliant!'

'Come on, I'd better get down to Mum now.'

'OK,' Lucy replied, following Eleanor.

As she got to the door, Lucy instinctively glanced over her shoulder as a movement caught her eye. Her jaw dropped... *Ollie and Fred were waving goodbye!*

'*Look!*' she gasped to Eleanor, who turned her head... to see the bear and panda sitting motionless as before!

'What?'

'*Ollie and Fred – they were waving goodbye to you!*'

'Ha ha, I'm really going to miss your little jokes.'

'*No, honest, they were!*'

'So you must come to see me as soon as you can.'

'But...'

'Come on, my mum's waiting.'

★★★

As they made their way downstairs, the girls heard the sound of their mums chatting in the living room and realised they were talking about them.

'When you think, they've been friends virtually since the day they were born,' Eleanor's mum was saying.

'Yes, literally; I'm sure there aren't many friends

around who were born on the same day in the same hospital,' Lucy's mum replied.

'So they're bound to miss each other.'

'Yes, I'm sure they will.'

The girls looked at each other with sadness in their eyes as they heard this. It was true – they had been friends all of their lives, because, after they were born, the two mums became friends and met up every week for coffee.

'I used to like going to your house when I was little because you had better toys than me,' Lucy remembered.

'And I liked going to your house because you had a garden with a swing and a slide,' Eleanor replied.

'And don't forget the mini trampoline; I couldn't get you off that sometimes.'

'Hmm, yes, I remember that,' Eleanor sighed.

Reaching the bottom of the stairs, Lucy said, 'My mum's right you know, Elle, I will miss you terribly.'

'And my mum's right too, Lu, I'm going to miss you just as much.'

Although trying their very best not to, they both burst into tears and flung their arms around each other, squeezing so tight they could hardly breathe. The mums coming out into the hall gave each other a knowing look at the sight before them. Eleanor's mum then said, as delicately as she could, 'Time to go I'm afraid, Eleanor, if we leave now, we should be in Liverpool by supper-time.'

Hearing this, the girls slowly untangled, with Eleanor saying, 'Am I still having a sleep-over at Nanny and Grandad's tonight?'

'Yes, and Grandad's cooking your favourite for supper.'

'What, spaghetti with smoky tomato, and seafood sauce?'

'That's right, so come on, get your coat on and we'll be on our way.'

***

Lucy felt a sickening feeling in her stomach. *How can Eleanor be thinking of food at a time like this, is she really going to miss me?* she thought. *Will she forget me once she's left here? Will I ever see her again?*

Almost as if she could read her thoughts, Eleanor turned and said to her, 'Grandad should go on *Masterchef* because he's such a good cook and when you come and visit, I'm going to get him to cook it for you too.'

'Ooh, I'm looking forward to that,' Lucy said, cheering up.

'Now we'll keep in touch and, as soon as we're settled in, we'll invite you up, OK, Lucy?' said Eleanor's mum, Sam, as they made their way to the door.

'OK,' Lucy replied with a smile, but with sudden thoughts of other friends who had left her school promising to keep in touch entering her head. She reached out for Eleanor's hand and held it tight as they walked in silence out to Betty. On reaching the car she said, 'Do you remember Eveen and Neeve who were with us in first year?'

'Oh yes, I do – they were the twins who we joked had back to front names; they left when their parents went on a mission to Kosovo, didn't they?'

'That's right. They promised to keep in touch, but they never did.'

'Ah, but they weren't special friends, not like you and I are, Lu; we'll be friends for ever, won't we?'

'Yes we will,' Lucy nodded keenly, reassured by her friend's reply.

They then gave each other a final hug, before Eleanor got in the front passenger seat and closed the door. She wound down the window, and Lucy, for a final time, reached for her hand and squeezed it.

'I'll be nagging my mum every day to see if you've been in touch, so make sure you do, and soon,' she said.

'I will,' said Eleanor as the car engine spluttered noisily into life.

'Oh I *must* get that exhaust fixed,' Sam said in exasperation.

'Yes you must, Mum, it's so embarrassing – I feel ashamed!'

Lucy and her mum laughed at that remark, then stepped aside as the car was put into gear. They watched as it was driven a short distance, did a u-turn, and then drove back towards them, with hands being waved and goodbyes being shouted as it approached.

'Text me when you get there so we know you've arrived safely!' Lucy's mum, Louise, yelled back.

'OK, will do,' came back the reply. Then, with a final wink from Betty as she went over a speed bump, they were gone.

3

HORLA MAKES AN APPEARANCE

Tears started to form again in Lucy's eyes as the car disappeared from sight. Noticing this, her mum put her arms around her and said, 'Come on, darling, let's go inside and bake some cakes,' something they'd done together since Lucy was three, and she still enjoyed licking the spoons and whisks clean once mixing was complete.

'You start, Mum, I'll join you in a few minutes, I need to go to my room to put some things away,' she replied.

With that, she ran into the house, up the stairs and, remembering what had happened a few minutes earlier, walked slowly into her bedroom… to find Ollie and Fred back on sentry duty!

Confused and a little scared, Lucy walked to her dressing table and sat down with her back to the mirror. She stared closely at the bear and panda, standing motionless in their usual positions, and wondered how they had managed to move and wave their arms like they did.

It must have been Eleanor making it happen, she thought. *How else would they move? But how did she do it? How did she make them wave when she was almost out the door?*

Puzzled, and without an answer, Lucy's thoughts drifted to how school would be from now on without her best friend. Neither of them had ever been ill, so there hadn't been a single school day – apart from the Coronavirus lockdown – when they weren't together, either working in the classroom or playing; it was going to be very different at school without her.

She thought of the other friends she had, like Tallulah. She was very nice but spent most of her time practising the hula-hoop because she wanted to be a champion like a girl on YouTube, who could keep twenty hoops going at once.

She thought of Grace, who she got on fine with in class but never met out of school because she had a pony and was always too busy mucking it out.

'It's amazing how much poo comes out of my little pony,' she would often say.

And she thought of Bethany, who she played with at playtime, but who would get them both into trouble in the classroom with her constant chattering.

Yes, there are other nice girls in my class, but nobody as special as Eleanor, she thought. 'And I'm never going to see her again,' she found herself saying out loud as she quietly wept, feeling very lonely.

She turned and opened a drawer, pulling out a handkerchief to wipe her eyes. As she did so, a voice suddenly said, *'Hello!'*

Lucy was startled. She looked up and saw a blue-eyed, blonde-haired girl about her own age, staring at her from the mirror. She turned around quickly to face the girl whose reflection she had seen, thinking she was behind her, but to her surprise, she wasn't

there. She gasped in confusion and turned back to the mirror… to see the girl still staring at her.

'Don't be frightened! My name's Horla, will you be my friend?' the girl said.

It was now Lucy's turn to stare, open-mouthed, at the face looking out at her. She blinked twice, expecting her own reflection to suddenly reappear and everything be back to normal, but that didn't happen. Instead she noticed the wallpaper behind the girl; it was blue not yellow, and where were the posters of Princesses Elsa and Anna? It was then Lucy realised, *she was looking into the girl called Horla's bedroom!*

Her voice was shaking and, although she still wasn't sure if she was imagining it, she gulped and said quietly, 'Did you say your name is Horla?'

'Yes,' said the girl in the mirror, 'and yours is Lucy, isn't it?'

'Yes,' Lucy replied, wondering how she knew.

'Why were you crying?' said Horla from the mirror.

'Well I don't usually cry,' Lucy replied, trying to sound grown up, 'but I'm just so unhappy because my best friend Eleanor has gone to live far away and I'm *really* going to miss her.'

'Yes, I thought that was the reason. I heard you discussing it; she is very nice and I think I'd miss her too if she was my friend.'

'*What!*' said Lucy in a state of shock, 'You mean you were here when Eleanor was here?'

'Yes I was, and I could help you to see her again if you like.'

Lucy looked at her with a puzzled expression on her face.

'*How*?' she said.

'Well, I can *do* things,' replied Horla, smiling rather confidently.

Lucy thought, as she said this, how alike the girl was to herself, and how she even wore her hair in plaits like she did.

'What sort of things?' she asked, puzzled by Horla's statement.

'Well, for one thing, I can travel very fast if I want to.'

Lucy, about to ask another question, then heard a voice shouting, 'Horla, come down now please.'

'Whoops, I'll have to go,' Horla then said, 'my mum is calling me, speak to you soon; bye, and bye to you too, Ollie and Fred.'

Lucy automatically glanced across at her two large cuddly toys and her eyes nearly popped out of her head – they were waving goodbye to Horla who, along with her bedroom, suddenly disappeared, leaving Lucy staring open-mouthed at her own reflection.

***

Lucy sat for a few minutes, staring at herself in the mirror.

Am I going mad? she thought, *Did I just imagine all that?*

Slowly, she went across to Ollie and Fred and looked at them suspiciously. Feeling a little nervous, she poked them with her right forefinger, as if expecting an electric shock. As nothing happened, she cautiously picked them up one at a time and examined them. They were certainly no different than they had always been, so how had they been able to wave? She just couldn't work it out.

'There's something strange going on around here,' she said to Fred. 'And you can wipe that silly grin off your face,' she said to Ollie, 'you're in on this too!'

But Ollie and Fred didn't bat an eyelid. A sudden chill went down her spine; she felt as if she was in the middle of a movie that was about to get scary, and her mind started to wander.

Maybe toys are about to take over the world! Maybe there are skeletons now hanging in my wardrobe instead of dresses, she thought, horrified, but not daring to look. She froze, wondering what to do next, when a voice almost made her jump out of her skin.

'Lucy, there's some licking to do,' her mum was shouting up to her.

'OK, Mum, I'm coming,' she shouted back, relieved to be back in the real world. She hurried downstairs to the kitchen and burst in shouting, 'Mum, Mum, you'll never believe what's just happened: I've been talking to a girl in my dressing table mirror!' Immediately as she said it, she realised how ridiculous it sounded, and wasn't surprised when her mum burst out laughing.

'No, honest, Mum, I *really was* talking to a girl in the mirror, her name's Horla and she said she could help me get to see Eleanor.'

'Oh and how does she propose to do that?' her mum replied.

'She said she can travel really fast and…' her voice trailed off, as it was obvious from the look on her mum's face that she thought she was making it up.

'Oh, Lucy, you've always had such a great imagination,' she said smiling, 'I remember when you were little you would have two-way conversations with Ollie.'

'What do you mean two-way conversations?'

'You would speak to him then answer yourself back, pretending it was Ollie answering.'

'Really?'

'Yes, you thought of Ollie as a ferocious grizzly bear and tried to sound like one.'

'And did I?'

'No, you sounded more like Peppa Pig, but at least it showed you had imagination.'

'I didn't imagine the girl in the mirror though, Mum.'

'That's OK, sweetheart. Now when you've done your licking, put everything straight into the sink for washing.'

4

LUCY'S NOT BELIEVED

A short while later, and after the scrumptious task of removing the cake mix from the utensils, Lucy went back upstairs to her room. She stared at Ollie and Fred as she entered, wondering if they had been up to anything while she had been out of the room, but they were in exactly the same position as when she left. She then sat for ten minutes looking into the mirror at her own reflection... and nothing happened. She hadn't imagined it, she knew she hadn't. Then she heard the sound of her dad coming in and rushed downstairs to greet him.

'Dad, you'll never believe what happened, I mean I hope you *do* believe what happened,' she blurted

out without pausing for breath. 'A girl appeared in my mirror and was talking to me.'

'Hang on, slow down,' Dad said, 'what do you mean, a girl appeared in your mirror and was talking to you?'

At that moment, her mum came into the hall and raised her eyebrows as her husband looked at her for an explanation.

'I think she's already missing Eleanor,' she mouthed to him.

Lucy noticed this and said, 'Honest Dad, I have, her name's Horla and she said she wants to be my friend.'

'OK, OK, but where is she now, this girl called Horla?'

'I don't know, she said she had to go because her mum was calling her, so she waved goodbye to me, then to Ollie and Fred, who waved back, and then she disappeared.'

At this point, her dad, and her mum who hadn't heard the bit about Ollie and Fred waving, burst into shrieks of laughter. Her dad then picked her up, gave her a cuddle and said, 'I know what you're doing; you're rehearsing for a school play aren't you? And you're doing a very good job too!'

'No I'm *not,* Dad; I'm *not* rehearsing for anything. I *did* see a girl in my mirror,' Lucy pleaded.

'I'll tell you what,' Dad responded, 'you show me this girl in the mirror and then I'll believe you; come on, let's go to your room now.'

So Lucy, her mum and dad went up to her bedroom and looked in the mirror, for two minutes... and saw only themselves!

'So, what did she look like, this mystery girl in the mirror? Was she small like you are, or tall like Eleanor?' Dad said.

'Well I couldn't tell how tall she was, but she was about my age and she was blonde with blue eyes; oh, and she wore her hair in plaits.'

'Oh really, and what is the colour of your hair?'
'Blonde.'

'And what is the colour of your eyes?'
'Blue.'

'And you don't by chance have your hair in plaits at the moment do you?'

'Yes,' Lucy replied in a low voice, realising what her dad was getting at. She started to feel a little foolish. Doubt came into her head again, and she thought once more that maybe she had imagined it all, that there never was a girl in her mirror, and that Ollie and Fred never waved goodbye. And then she remembered how Ollie and Fred had suddenly appeared on the seats while she and Eleanor were looking out of the window, something she blamed Eleanor for doing.

I am not imagining it, it did happen, she convinced herself subconsciously, then made up her mind: if Horla, the girl in the mirror, did come back asking to be her friend, then she would be... but she wouldn't tell anyone else about her. No, Horla would be her friend... her secret friend.

'OK, I own up, I *was* making it up,' Lucy said suddenly, 'but I'm not rehearsing for a school play; I want to be a writer when I grow up, that's all. What I told you was pretty imaginative, don't you think?' she added with a smile on her face.

'Well, yes, a bit far-fetched, but imaginative,' said Dad, nodding his head

'Thank goodness for that,' said Mum, 'for a moment I thought you were going bonkers.'

***

That night, after her dad had kissed her goodnight and left the room, Lucy got up to look in the mirror once more, having already done so several times in the last few hours.

'Where are you, Horla, where are you?' she whispered, desperately hoping for a face to appear, a face that she had to confess, did look a bit like her. She waited and waited, until finally, with tiredness overcoming her, she got back into bed, propped herself up with a pillow, and continued staring in the direction of the dressing table, wondering again if she had imagined it all.

Her eyelids felt like heavy weights as she fought to stay awake; closing, then opening, closing, then opening. Eventually, though, sleep won the battle, but just before it did, her eyes opened one last time and she smiled, then, like a drawbridge on a castle, her eyes closed and she drifted off to dream... of Horla, the girl in the mirror.

Horla smiled too. 'Night night, Lucy,' she whispered. 'Sleep tight, and don't let the bed-bugs bite!'

5

THE MYSTERY OF THE HAIRBRUSH

The following day was Monday, and Lucy woke up to the sound of her mum's voice.

'Come on, sleepy head, it's time to get up, you don't want to be late for school,' she said, walking over and opening the bedroom curtains. As she did so, Lucy, bleary-eyed though she was, noticed that it seemed to be slightly brighter outside than normal. Then Mum added, 'And there is a surprise for you outside, come and have a look.'

Lucy jumped out of bed and went to the window – to find everywhere covered in snow. Her mum looked at her, expecting to see an excited face – but Lucy looked far from excited.

'Aren't you pleased? I thought you loved snow,' she said.

'I do love snow, Mum…I just don't like being hit by snowballs, that's all.'

'Oh toughen up, Lucy, it is only snow; it doesn't come very often so enjoy it while you can.'

'It's all right for you, Mum… you're not the one getting pelted with them.'

'Oh I had my fair share of being hit by snowballs when I was your age, and it never did me any harm; if anyone throws a snowball at you, simply throw one back at them.'

'I can cope with one snowball, Mum, but sometimes it's a lot more than one.'

'Why, are people picking on you?'

'No, not really, Mum,' Lucy replied with a sigh.

'What does that mean, "No, not really?" Are they, or aren't they?'

'Well…'

'Well what?'

'Well they don't just pick on me.'

'Who, who are you talking about?'

'The Taylor triplets.'

'Oh, that lot! I believe they run riot on the street where they live.'

'Well it's not just on their street they run riot, they run riot in school as well… when the teachers' backs are turned that is. Last time it snowed they made a pile of snowballs and they bombarded me with them. I ended up being soaked right through to the skin; even my knickers were wet, although I don't know if the snow caused that or whether I'd wet myself with fright at seeing all those snowballs coming in my direction.'

'Did you tell your teacher?'

'No. When I said I was going to do that, they laughed and said they would beat me up if I did, so I didn't. I just sat in class in wet clothes till they dried out, then I caught a cold. Remember, you and Dad caught it off me.'

'Oh darling, you should have told us about that,' Mum said, putting her arm around her. 'You should never keep that sort of thing to yourself.'

'I know, Mum, but I didn't want you to cause a fuss in case they picked on me even more. The funny thing is, they never pick on me when Eleanor is around.'

'That's because they're bullies, and like all bullies they're cowards too. I'll bet they only target children who are small like you.'

'They do, and they pick on the first years too.'

'I thought as much. People like that never pick on someone their own size, which Eleanor was.'

Lucy felt a sudden pang of loneliness. Her mum saying, "Eleanor was", although not intentional, was a further reminder that her best friend, who always stuck up for her, was a long, long way from her now.

★★★

A short time later, Lucy was downstairs eating her usual cereal and toast, and mulling over the events of the previous day. She had made up her mind not to mention the girl in the mirror again when, suddenly, she heard a noise coming from upstairs: it was as if something had been dropped onto the floor of her bedroom. Her mum heard it too and looked puzzled; *they were the only ones in the house, so what could have made that noise?* they both thought.

'Something must have fallen, although goodness knows what,' said Mum. 'I'll go and investigate.'

'Hang on, I'll come with you,' said Lucy.

So upstairs they went to Lucy's room. At a glance everything seemed to be in place, and there certainly wasn't anything on the floor. As her mum moved around looking, Lucy thought she detected a slight movement out of the corner of her eye and looked in Ollie's direction – but he was perfectly still.

'Well nothing seems to have fallen down here; let's have a look in the other bedrooms,' said Mum.

Lucy followed her around each room upstairs; they even looked in the bathroom and toilet, but found nothing that could have made the noise. Then her mum thought she had the answer.

'I've got it,' she said, 'it will have been an airlock.'

'An airlock, what's an airlock?' Lucy queried.

'It's when air gets in the water pipes.'

'Really; how does it get there?'

'Well, that careless father of yours changed a washer on a tap last night; it must have happened then.'

'Oh, right,' Lucy replied with a smile, remembering Dad was in the doghouse with her mum.

Satisfied with her explanation, Lucy's mum proceeded back down the stairs, but instead of following her, Lucy stepped into her bedroom once more. She had thought earlier that something about her dressing table wasn't quite right, but what? Then it dawned on her – she was left-handed and always, without fail, put her hairbrush down to the left of the mirror when she finished with it, but her hairbrush was now to the right of the mirror.

The hairbrush, that's what made the noise we heard downstairs, I'm sure of it, she thought, *it's been knocked onto the floor and then picked up again.*

Her stomach started doing somersaults with excitement, more convinced than ever she hadn't imagined the events of yesterday.

'Horla, are you there?' she whispered into the dressing table mirror, but just like the previous night, her own reflection continued gazing back at her. She turned and looked at Ollie and Fred who, instead of waving like they had the previous day, stood motionless like stuffed toys do.

'Horla,' she whispered once more, but still the girl in the mirror didn't appear. She waited, her mind drifting back to yesterday.

I did not imagine it, she thought once again, *she spoke to me and I spoke to her, she knew my name and she even knew of Eleanor and said she'd help me see her again, so I couldn't have imagined it.* 'Oh come on Horla, *please,*' she pleaded.

Suddenly, the sound of her mum's voice brought her back to reality: 'Come and finish your breakfast Lucy; you don't want to be late for school.'

'OK, Mum, I'm coming,' she reluctantly replied, and, with a final glance at the hairbrush, made her way back downstairs.

6

THE SNOWFALL AND BOOMERANG PASTY

At 8.45am, Lucy got dropped off at school by her mum. As she walked to the gates her heart sank, for fast approaching her from behind were the Taylor triplets: Tayler, Tillie and Tulip. They were much bigger than her and *very, very,* horrible, especially Tayler Taylor, a nasty piece of work if ever there was one. They weren't identical triplets, and they never dressed alike, although they did all wear their hair in ponytails. Some children said that suited them as they looked like ponies, all three having big eyes and protruding teeth, although others said that was being unkind to ponies.

Lucy quickened her pace, but then the Taylors

broke into a run and within seconds they were passing her, laughing out loud, as Tayler Taylor squirted orange juice on the back of Lucy's coat. Lucy then slowed down and walked cautiously up the path. She noticed that the three bullies were making snowballs and they were making them really, really hard so that they would really, really hurt, and, they put small stones inside so they hurt even more!

Tillie Taylor noticed her first and said, 'Look – it's Juicy Lucy, and she hasn't got her bodyguard with her.'

Lucy didn't know why she called her "Juicy Lucy", but she knew she was in trouble.

If only Polo would walk around the corner now, I would be OK, she thought, but the headmaster wasn't around, and she knew she couldn't turn back. Then she gained a bit of confidence as she was joined by Bethany and Grace, although they looked as frightened as she was, so they all walked up together, trying not to look afraid. As they got closer, Tillie and Tulip Taylor, egged on by Tayler Taylor, who was keeping a lookout for teachers, picked up a snowball in each hand, ready to take aim. Lucy and the girls started to run. Then Tayler Taylor shouted, '*NOW!*' and their arms went right back so they could throw the snowballs really hard.

Lucy was just about to duck when a strange, loud noise made her look upwards to see what she

described to her mum later as the funniest sight she had ever seen: a massive pile of snow was falling off the roof and it landed right on top of the triplets, then, peering out from under it, appeared their three snow-covered heads, with eyes blinking and mouths spluttering, as they tried their best to free themselves. The snow was everywhere: in their hair and in their ears, inside their coats and in their wellingtons.

A crowd soon gathered, all laughing and giggling at what they saw. Lucy then heard someone giggling behind her, but when she turned around there was nobody there. A strange feeling suddenly came over her; she realised she had heard that giggle before, in fact she had heard it only yesterday!

*** ★★★

Before long it was time for lunch. As she was tucking in, Lucy noticed the Taylors looking across at her and hoped they hadn't seen her laugh at them that morning. Tayler Taylor, who was always the one to start trouble, had a pasty in her hand and didn't look as if she was about to eat it. Tayler watched to see which way Mrs. O'Connor, the teacher on duty, was looking, and when she looked the other way, Tayler hurled the pasty really fast in Lucy's direction. Lucy saw it coming and ducked, but she needn't have done, because a very strange thing happened: the pasty suddenly turned, like a boomerang, and headed even faster back towards Tayler Taylor who hadn't time to even *think* of ducking before it went *SPLAT*, right into her face.

It was a very juicy pasty with lots of vegetables and gravy, and she had sweet corn and potato in her hair, a baby carrot sticking out of an ear, a pea stuck up her nose and gravy running off her chin; it was such a funny sight that everyone was laughing at her, even her sisters. Then Lucy heard a little giggle coming from over her right shoulder and turned, but again there was nobody there. Lucy smiled with excitement; she knew it was that same giggle she had heard earlier and in her bedroom the previous day… and she knew it was Horla doing the giggling!

HORLA EXPLAINS
HER POWERS

That afternoon, Lucy's mum picked her up from school as usual, and in the car Lucy excitedly told her all about the snow falling off the roof onto the 'Terrible Taylor triplets' and about the boomerang pasty, including the bit about the pea up Tayler Taylor's nose and the baby carrot sticking out of her ear.

'Here we go again,' her mum sighed, 'you and your imagination; I'm beginning to think that you *should* become a writer when you grow up – you'd be very good at it!'

'But honest, Mum, it happened,' Lucy replied, although she didn't say why she thought it had happened. She'd guessed it was Horla, the girl in the mirror, who was behind it all, but she wasn't going to bring *that* subject up again. They hadn't believed her yesterday, so why would her parents believe her today.

When they arrived home, Lucy went straight to the bathroom. As she turned on the tap to wash her hands, a voice suddenly said, 'Wasn't that fun today?'

Lucy's eyes immediately shot to the mirror, and there, staring back at her with a big grin on her face, was the girl called Horla. Lucy was excited – and relieved; she knew she hadn't imagined it, Horla *was* real……*well, sort of.*

'So you *were* there!' she exclaimed in a rather louder voice than she realised.

'What was that you said?' shouted her mum from the kitchen.

'Nothing, Mum,' Lucy replied.

Both girls then put their fingers to their lips and said, 'Shush!' at the same time. Then Lucy said, 'I *thought* you were there, I heard you laughing when the snow fell onto the Taylor triplets.'

'Actually, Lucy, it didn't fall, I made it drop on to them.'

'*Did you?*' Lucy replied, amazed.

'Yes.'

'And the pasty hitting Tayler Taylor in the face, did you do that too?'

'Yes.'

'Wow that is awesome.'

'Do you think so?'

'Yes, in fact it's mega-awesome.'

'Stop it – you'll have me blushing.'

'But how, I mean, how did you do it?'

'Oh, it's quite easy really, I just think about it and it happens.'

Lucy was dumbstruck. 'You just think about it and it happens!' she gasped.

'Yes.'

'Whoa,' Lucy whispered, taking that statement in. Then she asked, 'How come you were there but I couldn't see you? In fact, nobody could see you.'

'Oh, that's simple,' Horla replied, 'when I come into your world I become invisible.'

'Wow, cool!' said Lucy, confused. 'But what do you mean, when you come into my world, don't you live here too?'

'No, actually, I don't,' said Horla.

That answer really left Lucy baffled.

'Well,' she paused, 'if you don't live here, then where do you live?'

Suddenly, before Horla could answer, Lucy's mum's voice echoed from the kitchen.

'Lucy, snacks are ready,' she shouted.

'Oh,' Lucy said, 'I'd better go; will you come back later and you can tell me then?'

'Yes I will, to your bedroom mirror after your snack?'

'Yes, OK, I won't be too long.'

'OK, see you then.'

'OK, bye.'

Lucy dried her hands and rushed to the kitchen with a huge grin on her face – she'd never been so excited!

'You know, if I didn't know better, I'd think you had a friend in that bathroom,' her mum said, smiling as she walked in.

'Don't be silly, Mum, I'm just feeling happy that's all.'

'That's good, because you were far from happy this morning.'

'Well a lot of things have happened since then, Mum.'

'Hmm, so your imagination would have us believe.'

Lucy laughed; she didn't care if her mum believed her or not, she knew that it *had* all happened, and that's what mattered.

***

Later in her bedroom, Lucy continued with her questioning.

'So come on Horla, tell me where *do* you live?'

Horla puffed out her chest proudly and replied, 'Well my dad says we live in a parallel world to yours.'

'What does that mean?' said a, by now, totally confused Lucy.

'Well, he says it's the same as yours, and is right next to yours, but the two worlds are invisible to each other. He says that millions and millions of years ago there was a big bang and one world split in to two making yours and ours; we are about seventy years behind now though, well in inventions at least – we haven't even been to the moon yet.'

Lucy didn't want Horla to think she was stupid so she just said, 'Oh I see.'

'Do you?' said Horla, surprised, 'Because I don't.'

'Well no, I don't either actually, it's probably something we'll understand when we're grown-ups,' Lucy replied.

'Yes, I suppose you're right,' said Horla.

'Anyway, what's your world called?'

'Ivarnio.'

'Ivarnio?'

'That's right, Ivarnio.'

'I've never heard of Ivarnio!'

'Well you might not have heard of it, but it exists, and that's where I'm speaking to you from right now.'

'But how come you are here in my mirror?'

'Well you see, on Sunday, *my* best friend, Carar, moved far away too. I knew she was going and that I would miss her a lot, so before she went I decided to try to contact someone in your world who was just like me who I could become friends with. I knew my dad had done it, and he's now got a very nice friend called Tristan who we both go and visit. So I sat in front of the mirror like he did and concentrated.

I wish I could meet someone just like me, I thought in my head, and then suddenly you appeared, looking very like me; you've even got plaits like me. I thought it would be difficult to do, but it wasn't. The strange thing is, everything seems so familiar, I don't know why. Anyway, I didn't let you see me at first as I didn't want to frighten you. I sort of knew what was going to happen – your best friend would be leaving too, and you were going to feel a little bit lonely just like me, so I hung around for a while and watched you – not to pry, you understand, just to make sure you were someone I would like; I hope you don't mind.'

'No, I don't mind at all, in fact I'm really glad you did.'

'Actually, I also came into your room; I hope you don't mind that either.'

'Ah ha, so it was *you* who moved my hairbrush.'

'Oh yes, that was clumsy of me, I knocked it on the floor by accident and it made quite a racket.'

'Hmm, well, it wouldn't have done had my carpet been down.'

'Why, where is it?'

'Dad dropped a tin of paint on it and it's gone to the tip, my new one's coming tomorrow and was very expensive apparently; Dad's really in the doghouse with Mum over it.'

'He's in the doghouse with your mum?'

'Yes.'

'Really?'

'Yes.'

'Well I didn't know you had a dog; I mean, how big is it – this dog – can your mum and dad really fit in its house?'

'No, no, you don't understand, I haven't got a dog… that's just an expression we use when, for example, a person is upset with another person – Mum's *very* upset with Dad because he should have put a dust sheet down before he started painting.'

'Oh, I see… so you haven't got a dog?'

'No.'

'An enormous dog?'

'No.'

'One that's so big it needs its own house?'

'Ha ha, no I haven't.'

'One so big, that its head sticks out the chimney pot?'

'No definitely not.'

'Phew, just as well; imagine the size of its p-double-o… you'd have to follow it with a wheelbarrow every time you took it to the park!'

Lucy laughed. 'So you don't use that expression where you come from?' she said.

'Oh cracker-doo-doos, no, we *never* use silly expressions; adults living in dogs' houses, for goodness sake... whoever heard such a thing!'

Lucy stared at Horla, suspecting her leg was being pulled. And she was right. Unable to sustain it any longer, Horla smiled.

'I'm only teasing, we do use that expression; my dad's always in the doghouse, in fact he spends so much time there that he pays rent!'

Lucy smiled as Horla continued, 'It's true; he's looking for furniture for it now!'

'Oh Horla, you're a nutcase, you really are!'

'It takes one to know one, Lucy. Anyway, as I was saying before, shortly after I replaced the hairbrush you and your mum came in; I kept perfectly still and tried not to make another noise – but then I had to move because your mum nearly trod on my toe.'

'Did she?'

'Yes, and then I trod on Ollie's foot, but fortunately neither of you noticed.'

'Ah, that explains it – I *thought* he moved, but I didn't say anything to Mum because she doesn't believe anything I say anymore; when I told her about the snow falling off the roof and the pasty turning around and going back to where it came from, she just said I'm imagining things – so how did you do that?'

'I told you earlier, I just think about it and it happens,' Horla said casually, as if it was the most natural thing in the world to do.

'So I *wasn't* imagining it when I saw Fred and Ollie waving goodbye to you?'

'No, you weren't; they did actually wave, didn't you boys?'

Lucy's eyes instinctively turned to her two sentries who were nodding their heads vigorously in agreement.

'Oh that is *so* creepy. I'll be having nightmares about my toys coming alive and wandering around my bedroom while I'm asleep.'

'Ha ha, no, that can't happen; they only come alive when I make them.'

'*Phew*, thank goodness for that. And the... *ahem*... very loud noise normally associated with people's bottoms?'

'Oh yes, that was me too. I couldn't resist it when you both denied ever doing it.'

'Gosh, and can everyone do these things where you come from?'

'Farting?'

'Well... *ahem,* we don't say that, we say trumping.'

'Trumping, why on Ivarnio do you call it trumping?'

'Dad says it's called after an American President, who could play the American National Anthem with his bottom.'

'*Could he?*'

'Yes, and he says the Queen plays a tune called "Rule Britannia" on hers.'

'*Phew*, it must take a lot of practice.'

'That's what I was thinking.'

'I'd rather learn the piano!'

'Yes me too.'

'Anyway; farting, trumping, call it what you like, yes, everyone can do that where I come from.'

'Actually, Horla, I meant *everything else* you can do.'

'Oh sorry, no, only me, my dad and my grandad, at least we think we're the only ones; Dad says I've inherited it from him and he inherited it from Grandad.'

'That's amazing, but why only you three?'

'Well Grandad always says it's because we are able to use all of our brain, whereas other people can only use a small part of theirs, although Dad says that's just a myth, so I don't really know.'

Lucy paused for a moment, taking in that fact, and then said, 'How did you know where my school was?'

'I didn't, I went there in your mum's car.'

Lucy gasped. *'You went there in my mum's car?'*

'Yes, I was sitting right next to you,' Horla explained. 'She's a very good driver isn't she; my mum hates driving in the snow.' Looking rather pleased with herself, she carried on, 'It's the first time I've come without Dad to look after me; I can't wait till he gets home so I can tell him about it.'

'What, you come here with your dad?' said Lucy, surprised.

'Yes, we go to football matches together, in fact, he scores goals in matches we go to. Years ago, his favourite player was somebody famous called Lionel Beckham, but he wouldn't have been famous without Dad.'

'How do you mean?'

'Well, whenever he tried to score goals the ball would always be going past the goal but Dad would make it bend and go into the net. Now he goes to loads of football matches to help footballers score goals. I sometimes score too, although the first time I tried, the ball hit the referee and knocked him out; now to get it right I really concentrate, like at school when we're having a test.'

'Oh, I hate tests.'

'Yes, so do I… but… if you and your dad come here…'

'And my grandad comes too.'

'Oh, and your grandad… how do you know nobody else from Ivarnio comes here?'

'We don't. We can see each other when we are on Earth so we know we would be able to see anyone else from Ivarnio, but the problem is, we don't know who is and who isn't. Dad says that when he first came here he noticed some people wearing clothes like we wear – what you would call a bit old fashioned – and he walked alongside them and asked if they were from Ivarnio, but they just looked around, wondering where the voice had come from. That's why we think we're the only ones, although we can't be sure.'

'They could have got modern clothes from here so they wouldn't stand out.'

'*What?* They'd stand out all right, we're invisible to people on Earth, remember… the clothes would be walking around without bodies!'

'Whoops, I forgot about that… but hang on… how come you're wearing modern clothes like me?'

'Because I told Dad how I liked what children on Earth were wearing and he had them made for me – now I'm a bit of a trend-setter.' Lucy smiled as Horla continued, 'Grandad says we shouldn't really interfere with what's happening on Earth though, and I think he's right, although I'm sure it's OK to score the odd goal at a football match and help if someone's getting bullied like you were today.'

'Oh yes, I agree; everyone likes seeing goals scored, and the Taylors are always picking on people and deserve a taste of their own medicine.'

'Yes they do, but I bet they never thought *they'd* be picked on – especially not by a pasty,' Horla joked.

'Oh that was *so* funny – did you see the look on Tayler Taylor's face as it did a U-turn and flew back at her?'

'I did; her eyes were bigger than saucers.'

'That's right, and her mouth was like an open bread bin; oh I wish we had a photograph of her like that.'

'Yes, and we could send it off to a publisher to be put on the cover of a scary book.'

Lucy laughed and said, 'Great idea – it could be called, *The Revenge of the Pasty*, and have pasties flying out of the baker's and hitting people who had eaten their pasty relatives.'

'Gosh Lucy, you've got a weird imagination; I expect you'd like custard pies to come flying out into people's faces too.'

'Even better,' Lucy chuckled, imagining the scene, but before she could say any more they heard footsteps coming up the stairs.

'Sounds like Mum so you'd better go. Will you come back later?'

'OK,' said Horla quietly, 'see you later.'

'OK,' Lucy whispered back, then, as Horla disappeared from the mirror, she picked up her hairbrush and started brushing her hair.

'Nearly time for tea, Lucy,' Mum said as she walked in. 'Can you give me a hand by laying the table and mashing the potatoes please?'

'OK, Mum,' Lucy replied, getting up from her seat, 'let's get a-laying and a-mashing!'

Her mum smiled and left the room, followed a few seconds later by Lucy, who, being in such a happy mood, stopped and waved to Fred and Ollie… who of course didn't wave back.

'Well please yourselves, boys,' she mouthed to them, then, nodding her head from side to side whispered, *'see if I care!'* She giggled then walked downstairs with a silly grin on her face thinking, *Hmm, maybe Horla's right, maybe I do have a weird imagination.*

8

DAD GETS A
BLOODY NOSE

Later, Lucy was really, really annoyed with herself
for telling her parents what had happened that day.
She realised that as neither of them had believed her
when she spoke about Horla the previous day, she
shouldn't have expected them to believe her when
she told them about what had happened today. But
it was too late – she *had* told Mum, and Mum had
told Dad, and Dad was winding her up about it – *and
getting her really irritated*.

'So tell me again about the remote control
pasties?' he said, mimicking falling backwards onto
the settee after being hit in the face by one.

They often had mock fights – possibly Dad's

attempt to toughen her up, so she jumped on top of him and started punching him... *really hard.* She was fed-up with them not believing her, and now, she'd decided, she didn't want them to believe her anyway. She'd never mention Horla, or anything that happened when Horla was around, *ever again.*

'Whoa, whoa, steady on, Little Miss,' Dad said, fending off the blows, 'what's got into you today?'

'I'm using my imagination again,' she said in frustration, 'I'm a boxer now and I'm going to beat you up.'

'What's going on in there?' Mum shouted from the sitting room on hearing the commotion.

'I'm bonding with our daughter,' Dad replied, trying his best not to get hit. Mum chuckled; she knew how much he enjoyed playing with Lucy – only this time Lucy wasn't playing! Blow after blow rained down on him and he loved every second of it – until Lucy punched him smack on the nose!

'Oh I'm sorry, Dad,' she said, shocked, as the blood started flowing out of both nostrils and into his mouth. She'd never ever hurt him before and rushed for a box of tissues fearing her pocket money was in jeopardy, but she needn't have worried.

'Brilliant right hook, Lucy, but next time you must follow it up with a left,' Dad said, taking the tissues off her to stem the flow of blood. 'I'll make a boxer of you yet!'

Gosh, if Horla thinks I'm weird, Lucy thought, *I wonder what she'd make of Dad!*

'I'm really sorry about that, Dad,' she replied, realising the time, 'but I'm off to do my homework now.'

Dad wrinkled his forehead in surprise; he'd never known her be keen to do homework before.

'OK Champ, see you later,' he said. Then, with a tissue sticking out of each nostril, he made his way to the bathroom to mop up the blood.

***

Upstairs in her bedroom, Lucy started on her homework. Soon, to her delight, Horla reappeared in the mirror saying, 'Hi Lucy, has Eleanor been in touch yet?'

'No, Horla, not yet, but her mum texted to say they had arrived without any problem, which is surprising when you think of the racket Betty was making when they set off.'

'Well *you* could contact *her.*'

'I suggested that, but Mum says to be patient and Eleanor will get in touch with me eventually.'

'And then we could go and see her?'

'Oh, Horla, what did you mean by that, you know, when you said yesterday that you would help me see her? Last night I dreamt you appeared in my mirror and we flew off to Liverpool in your very own plane.'

'Ha ha, don't be silly, little girls don't own planes.'

'I know, it was just a dream, but you did say you could travel very fast.'

'Well I can, but not by plane.'

'Don't tell me – you own a racing car!'

'No, I don't own a racing car; my feet wouldn't reach the pedals if I did!'

'You own a motorbike then?'

'No, I don't own a motorbike.'

'Surely you couldn't possibly own a train?'

'That would be ridiculous.'

'No more ridiculous than sitting in your bedroom talking to someone in a parallel world!'

'Ha ha, that's true.'

'Oh, Horla, you couldn't possibly, could you...?'

'Couldn't possibly what?'

'Well, *ahem*... you don't sprout wings when you come into our world do you?'

'Oh cracker-doo-doos, and here's me thinking the plane idea was ridiculous; no, I do not sprout wings... what do you think I am, a talking seagull in disguise?'

'No, I was only joking.'

'*Phew*, thank goodness for that!'

'Anyway, I've worked out that you don't travel fast by plane or train or car or motorbike or wings, so I give in now; tell me, how are we going to get to see Eleanor?'

Horla laughed and said, 'If I tell you, Lucy, you won't believe it, so I think it is best you wait and see!'

9

THE GIRLS
NEED A PLAN

At school, Lucy made mental notes about things that happened during the day so she had plenty to chat about when she got together with Horla in the evening. She would talk about her classmates, most of whom were normal, plus the odd one she wasn't so sure about – like Bob, or "Bob the Rob", as some people called him. She explained how, since his arrival a few months earlier, things had started to go missing from the classroom and her classmates had suspected it was Bob who was taking them.

'Little things like rubbers, pencils, pencil sharpeners and pencil cases, and last night Bethany arrived home to discover that a very nice pen she got for Christmas was missing from her bag. We can't be certain it's him taking them of course, because we haven't any proof, but it's strange that it's only started to happen since he joined the class.'

At that point it was Horla's turn to make a mental note too: *"Bob the Rob",* was now firmly planted in her brain.

'What I'd really like to do,' she said, 'is come into your world again on my own, so you and I could play together.'

'Oh, that would be fun – but hang on, if you're invisible here, it might be a bit difficult to play with you when I can't see you.'

'Yes maybe,' said Horla pausing, 'but that might make it even more fun.'

Lucy thought for a moment and then said, 'Oh yes, we could get up to all sorts of tricks, or at least you could!'

'What sort of tricks do you have in mind?'

'Oh, I don't know, maybe you could walk behind people and pinch their bottoms.'

'Pinch their bottoms!' exclaimed Horla, 'I can't go round pinching people's bottoms.'

'Yes you can! It would be fun; think of the surprised look on their faces as they turn round to find there's nobody there, or better still, do it when somebody is close by so they get the blame.'

Horla laughed at the thought, then, seeing

where Lucy was coming from, said, 'If it's looks of surprise you're after, I could go into a greengrocer's and juggle some tangerines. I did that while Dad's back was turned the last time we came, but then he noticed people pointing, open-mouthed, and caught me in the act. He thought it was quite funny actually, but told me not to do it again – but as he wouldn't be around this time…'

'Ha ha, that sounds brilliant. Then we could go in to a supermarket and you could push a trolley up and down the aisles; people's eyes would be out on stalks on seeing that!'

'Yes they would, but why just push it when I could fill it as well?'

'Oh even more brilliant; I would so look forward to that!'

'And you could do things too,' Horla then remarked.

'Me?'

'Yes.'

'What could *I* do?'

'You could do magic tricks.'

'Oh I'm hopeless at doing magic tricks; I got a box of magic tricks for Christmas and couldn't get any of them to work.'

'No, you wouldn't be doing the magic – it would just *look* like you were.'

'Oh I get you… so I could, say, erm… let me think… I know, tell everyone I've got magic skates that follow me around, and then go out on my bike with you skating alongside me.'

'That's a brilliant idea.'

'And I could say my bike's magic too, and you could ride it while I use the roller skates.'

'Oh yes the opportunities for fun are endless, Lucy.'

'Hmm, yes, the problem is though, I never go out on my own, I'm always with other people so my parents might not let me do that.'

The girls sighed at the same time, both realising that their great idea wasn't that simple. However, they were desperate to meet up on Saturday, so it was left to Lucy to think of a good enough reason to go out alone without her parents being worried; she wasn't sure what reason she could give, but she was determined to think of something.

All week she racked her brains, until, waking up on Friday, she had what she thought was a good idea. The normal routine on a Saturday morning was for her and her mum to set off early to the shops where they collected the bread and papers. The smell from the local bakery was so inviting that a big queue would form outside by mid-morning, so they would always be there at 8.30am as the shop opened to buy what they needed; this usually included delicious rolls for lunch, exquisite croissants for Sunday breakfast, and Lucy's favourite, really tasty gingerbread men. They would also get whatever

Lucy's grandma wanted from the baker's and take it around to her, picking up newspapers from the paper shop on the way to her house a few roads away. Now if she could persuade her mum that this was something she could do on her own, her problem would be solved, she realised.

'Mum, I've been thinking,' she started off, 'it's silly for us both to go to the shops tomorrow, I can easily get the bread and papers for us *and* Grandma and take hers round to her on my own.'

'Good grief, what's brought that on?' her mum said in surprise.

'Nothing... it's just that I thought it would be a good idea really, I mean, you could get on with other things; you're always saying you've too much to do.'

'Well I do have a lot to do, but no darling, I don't think you should go to the shops on your own; you're much too young.'

'No I'm not; Emma, from my class, goes by herself and she's three weeks younger than me, *and* she's smaller than me too.'

'Hmm, that may be the case, but no, Lucy, I don't want you going to the shops, or anywhere else for that matter, alone, sorry.'

'But Mum...'

'No, sorry, that's final, when you're a bit older maybe, but not now.'

'But your jobs, you could be...'

'Forget about my jobs, darling… it's nice of you to think of me but I can manage.'

'But you've such a lot to do…'

'Look, I tell you what, if you really want to help, it can be your job to dry the dishes from now on, how about that?'

'Oh, Mum… why can't we use the dishwasher like everyone else?'

'Because it's not environmentally friendly, that's why – all that water and electricity; you know we only use it when we've had a lot of people round for dinner.'

Now Lucy was frustrated; not only had her plan failed, she'd been landed with the job of drying the dishes, something she hated doing because it was so boring. She couldn't help herself – in an annoyed voice, she muttered under her breath, *'Bloody dishes!'*

Her shocked mum, hearing this, said, 'Excuse me, but we speak the Queen's English in this house, *if you don't mind!'*

'What do you mean?' replied a sullen Lucy, realising she was being told off.

'I mean, you should speak like the Queen does.'

'Humph! I bet *she* says "bloody" when *she* dries the dishes!'

'No, I don't think so, the Queen always speaks properly even when she dries the dishes, and so should you.'

Now Lucy was really cheesed off and, with her head down, she got on with her breakfast in silence. Lucy's mum sat in silence too, with an image of the Queen drying the dishes in her head.

Lucy was disappointed and she knew Horla would be too.

There has to be a way of persuading Mum to let me go out alone, there just has to be, she thought in annoyance, but not a single bright idea came into her head then, or at school throughout the day.

***

'I don't suppose there'd be any point asking your dad for permission?' Horla said when they met up at the bathroom mirror after school.

'Nah, Dad's not the boss in our house, Mum is.'

'Hmm, it's the same in our house too.'

'So I don't know how I'm going to get out by myself tomorrow.'

'That's a pity – I was really looking forward to that.'

'So was I – I don't suppose you've any ideas, have you?'

'Well…' Horla hesitated.

'Well what?'

'Well… I *do* have an idea…'

'What sort of idea? Tell me quick before I go for my snack.'

'It's just something I could try that I know my dad can do, although he's told me not to try it till I'm older and more responsible, just in case anything goes wrong.'

'Oh flippin' heck, is it likely to go wrong?'

'There's only one way to find out.'

'Ooh, I'm not sure I like the sound of this.'

'Relax, it was just Dad being cautious, that's all; anything he can do I *should* be able to do, I mean, nothing I've done so far has gone wrong.'

'What about the time you knocked out the referee with a football?'

'Oh… that was just an accident – it was the first time I'd tried it and I'm much better at it now.'

'Hmm, well if you think it will work…'

'If it does, and I'm sure it will, it'll mean your mum gives you permission to go shopping alone tomorrow.'

'Oh that's fantastic.'

'It will be... if it works.'

'Oh Horla, you've just said you're *sure* it will work.'

'Well I'm pretty sure, but I won't know till I've done an experiment.'

'Lucy, will you stop talking to yourself and come and have your refreshments.' Lucy's mum's voice suddenly boomed from the dining room.

'Right, I'll go now but I'll see you after your snack, then I'll carry out the experiment,' Horla whispered, realising they'd been talking louder than they should have.

'OK, see you later,' Lucy whispered back, wondering what Horla meant by, "experiment". After washing her hands, she made her way to the dining room.

'Do you enjoy talking to yourself?' her mum asked as she walked in.

'Yes, I'm the only one I can get any sense out of,' Lucy replied, laughing.

Her mum laughed too, she was used to hearing that from her husband when he occasionally talked to himself.

'It must run in the family because your dad does that too.'

'Maybe he's not talking to himself, Mum, maybe he's got a secret friend.'

'Oh here we go again, you and your imagination – I can't wait till your first book is published.'

'Well actually, Mum, talking of books, our teacher, Mrs. Ardern, says that when people write books, they often write about their own experiences.'

'Hmm, that makes sense I suppose, writing about things they've actually seen happen.'

'Yes, that's what she says, so I was thinking, I could start my first book by writing about my experience going shopping alone tomorrow.'

'Oh, Lucy, don't you *ever* give up – I've told you, *no*.'

'It'd be a good experience for me though, Mum.'

'Oh yes, and a bad experience for me watching my hair turn grey with worry.'

'Actually, you already have a few grey hairs, Mum.'

'Be quiet!'

'No, you do, really.'

'Is it any wonder when I've got a daughter to look after, *and* she now wants to go out into the big wide world without me to look after her.'

'Oh cracker-doo-doos, Mum, I'd only be going to the baker's and the paper shop.'

'Cracker-doo-doos, what on earth does that mean?'

'Oh, erm, you know me and my imagination Mum, I sometimes say that instead of "flippin' heck".'

'Oh yes, you and your imagination; well I want you to imagine that you're *not* going out alone on Saturday, because that's exactly what's going to happen.'

'What… you mean I'm to imagine I'm *not* going out alone when really I am because you're going to let me?'

'No I am not going to let you, for goodness sake – now will you please drop this subject, it's wearing me out!'

'Sorry, Mum,' Lucy replied, realising her mum was a little upset.

Her mum looked over at Lucy and, feeling guilty, came over and put her arm around her, kissed her on the cheek and said, 'No, it's me who should be sorry for getting upset; actually, I'm quite proud of you having the confidence to go out alone, but let's leave it a little longer, OK?'

'OK, Mum,' Lucy sighed, 'we'll leave it a little longer.'

***

A short while later a rather downcast Lucy was in her room talking to Horla.

'Unless you can do something Horla, we won't be doing anything together tomorrow; Mum's being stubborn – wherever I go, she's going too.'

Horla smiled at her and said, 'Don't get too fed-up Lucy, we haven't tried the experiment yet, remember.'

Lucy suddenly perked up and said, 'Oh yes, I'd almost forgotten about that, yes you must do that, whatever it is.'

'OK, I will,' Horla said, smiling.

Lucy smiled back, anticipating once more seeing something out of the ordinary. Then she said, 'Just a moment,' and got up, closed the curtains and put on the light.

Horla giggled as she came back and sat down.

'What's so funny?' Lucy asked.

'Nothing,' Horla replied, doing her best not to laugh.

'There must be something.'

'No, there's nothing.'

Lucy looked at her suspiciously, then said, 'Anyway, what about this experiment, when are you going to do it?'

'I just have,' Horla replied.

'Oh great, and did it work?'

'Yes, it worked very well.'

'Fantastic, tell me what you did!'

Horla giggled once again and said, 'I made you close the curtains and put the light on.'

Lucy looked around gob-smacked – it was broad daylight, yet she *had* just closed the curtains and put the light on when there was absolutely no reason to do so.

'Flippin' heck, so I have,' she said.

'I thought I could do it, and I just have,' Horla said triumphantly.

Lucy slowly got up, still a little bewildered, and opened the curtains. She then switched the light back off and stood in silence for a few seconds, hardly believing what had just happened. Then she said, 'Hmm, that means that...'

'...I could persuade your mum to let you go out alone tomorrow? Yes, I think I could,' Horla said, finishing off Lucy's sentence.

'Cracker-flippin'-doo-doos,' Lucy replied, overjoyed, 'roll on tomorrow!

'Hang on, hang on, we've got to try it on your mum first, adult minds are harder for a child to control, Dad says, and I don't know how long I can make it last.'

'Oh right... hmm... so when are you going to try it?'

'Why not try it now? We don't want to leave it till tomorrow and find it doesn't work.'

'But I can't exactly invite her up here now, can I? She'd see you in the mirror!'

'Ah, but she wouldn't see me if I was in your house.'

'Oh right, well Mum's in the garden and the back door's wide open so you can sneak in now.'

'No, Lucy, I don't need to do that.'

'Don't you?'

'No – now stand back a moment.'

'OK,' said Lucy, wondering what the heck was going to happen next.

'Is this far enough?' she said, standing over by her bed.

'Yep,' replied Horla.

Lucy then watched, puzzled, as Horla's face moved closer to her own mirror, so close her nose was almost touching it. Then her face started to go out of shape as if it were on a flag that was slowly being waved.

Lucy then heard a low, creepy, sucking sound: *schlluuuuuuppppp* it went, sending a chill down her spine. She gulped as Horla's face distorted even more before vanishing completely, while several of the things from her dressing table fell onto the new carpet.

She started to feel very, very uneasy, and the imagination her parents had teased her about took over her head.

Oh no, I've been tricked, she thought, *I've fallen into a trap – Horla isn't a little girl at all; she's an alien who is about to take over my body. Then once she's done that, more aliens will come and take over my mum and dad, then Grandma, then they'll take over the world, and it's me that's let them do it… Oh what a stupid, stupid girl I've been!*

10

THE ALIEN IN
THE ROOM

Lucy was standing, open-mouthed, staring at the things on the floor, when suddenly she felt her hand being squeezed.

'Arrrrgggghhhh!' she screamed... but nothing came out of her mouth. She froze to the spot, petrified, thinking she'd been turned to stone; she desperately wanted her mum to walk into the room, but she was in the garden. Then she thought she heard a little giggle, so she whispered, ever so faintly, a tremble in her voice, 'Horla, w-w-where are you?'

'I'm here, right beside you,' a cheery Horla said, squeezing Lucy's hand once again.

Lucy turned in the direction of the voice, the distorted face still in her mind.

'What's up? You look like you've just seen a ghost!' Horla then said to her.

'*I wasn't frightened, I wasn't frightened,*' Lucy repeated, trying to sound brave.

'Well erm, you looked like you were, a bit,' Horla replied, doing her best not to laugh.

'*No I wasn't!*'

'But then, there was no need to be, was there?'

'*No, no there wasn't,*' Lucy replied shaking her head vigorously, 'it's just that… well… this is… I mean it's just… you're…'

'*Invisible?*' Horla laughed.

'Yes, well, I knew you would be but… well, I mean… like, having you stand next to me in my room, well… it's like a… well it's a million-trillion times awesome, that's what it is.'

Horla giggled at the exaggeration, and Lucy, now relaxing, realising that Horla wasn't an alien about to take over her body, gave a slightly nervous giggle too.

'Sorry, I forgot about telling you to move the things off the dressing table – that's how you heard me last time when your hairbrush fell onto the floor,' Horla then said.

'Well I'll know better for next time,' Lucy replied, about to bend down to pick them all up. Before she could reach them, the three doyleys lifted up into the air and flew across to the dressing table where the largest landed right in the centre and the other two landed either side of it.

She then stood, fascinated, as her trinket box and hairbrush, followed by her comb and hand-mirror, also rose into the air, then flew over and landed exactly where they had been before Horla came into the room – apart from the hairbrush of course; Lucy still hadn't got round to explaining she was left-handed!

'Wow,' Lucy said, amazed at what she had just seen, *'that was so cool.'*

'No, these are cool,' Horla said, picking up a doyley, 'it's nice to see these haven't gone out of fashion.'

'Well, actually, I hate to tell you this, but they have.'

'Why? Oh yes, I forgot, you're seventy years ahead of us, but then, how come you still have them?'

'Well apparently, when I was around three, and being looked after by Grandma while my parents were at work, I used to like nothing better than to sit in front of her bedroom mirror and brush and comb my hair using this set. One day she asked me if I would like them. I said, "Yes", and here they are, plus the doyleys that were with them at the time. I don't particularly like them now though – they are so old fashioned.'

'No they're not – every house has them where I come from.'

'Well I suppose every house here had them – *seventy years ago!'*

'OK, OK, I know we're old-fashioned compared to you but if you are ever thinking of getting rid of them, send them to Ivarnio – they'll find a good home there... not sure what the cost of a stamp would be though!'

'Oh very funny, and by the way, I'm left-handed you know.'

'Are you? So am I.'

'Then why did you put my hairbrush on the right-hand side of the dressing table?'

'Because I thought you'd be right-handed – everyone else I know is.'

'Hmm... so when you sat at your mirror and wished to meet someone just like you, it really worked, didn't it?'

'Wow, yes, I think you're right, it never occurred to me you'd be *very* like me though.'

'We could be mistaken for twins.'

'Yes we could... oh erm, no we couldn't, not when I can't be seen.'

'Whoops, forgot about that!'

'But... hmm, I wonder if I could experiment again and make you right-handed so we'd be that little bit different.'

'Don't you dare – I like me the way I am, thank you very much!'

'Ha ha, I was only kidding. C'mon, let's go into

the garden and see if your mum's up for a bit of "persuading".'

'OK, let's go.'

'No, not you two,' Horla then said, giggling again.

Lucy turned and gasped as she saw Ollie and Fred following them towards the door.

'I know I've said it before, but that is so creepy,' she said, watching them turn around and walk back again. 'Are you *sure* it's you that's making them do that?'

'Of course it is, isn't it boys?' she said to Ollie and Fred, who nodded their heads vigorously in agreement.

'There you are you see, you've absolutely nothing to worry about.'

Lucy shook her head and smiled at Horla's sense of humour.

'Come on, you inter-galactic nutcase,' she said, 'let's see if you can make my mum change her mind.'

***

As they walked downstairs, Horla said, 'Now, Lucy, I'll need to concentrate on your mum before you ask her anything, so, I'll go out first, you follow me a few minutes later, and hopefully this time she'll say yes.'

Lucy did as she was instructed and, after having a drink of water, she took a deep breath, crossed her fingers and went out into the garden.

'Hi darling,' her mum said on seeing her approach.

'Hi Mum.'

'Started your homework?'

'No, not yet, Mum.'

'Why haven't you? You know it's best to get it out of the way then you can relax for a few hours before bedtime.'

'Yes, I know that, but, it's just that I've been wondering, you know, if maybe you've changed your mind about me going to the shops tomorrow by myself.'

'Well it's funny you should say that, because that's exactly what I've just been thinking about.'

'Have you?'

'Yes, and do you know what, I *do* think it's a good idea and it *would* be a great help to me.'

'Oh that's great, Mum… and can I do it every week?'

'Yes, of course you can.'

'And Mum, if I did that, I wouldn't need to dry the dishes, would I?'

Mum hesitated for a moment, then said, 'Oh no, darling, there's no need for you to be drying dishes when you're helping me out by going shopping.'

Lucy felt her hand being squeezed, and squeezed Horla's back even tighter.

'Oh thanks, Mum,' she said, 'I'll go and get on with my homework now.'

'OK, you do that, and if you want me to check it, bring it to me and I will do.'

'Thanks, Mum – see you later.'

Both girls then trotted off, hand in hand, back to the house.

'*Yessss!*' Lucy said as they got back inside, 'I've got permission to go out alone on Saturday *and* I don't have to dry the dishes after all.'

'Whoa, you were pushing your luck there though; I wasn't expecting you to ask her *that* question.'

'Well, I just thought that as you'd put her in such a nice mood she'd agree with me – and she did.'

'I'm surprised you didn't ask her to raise your pocket money too.'

'Ha ha, now that *would* be pushing my luck!'

'Yes, I suppose so, but anyway, the most important thing is we are going out together tomorrow morning, *and* we're going to have some fun.'

'Oh yes, I'm so looking forward to that. In fact, now I wish it was for the whole day.'

'Ooh, that'd be brilliant.'

'Yes, I know.'

'Hmm, what we'd need for that is another plan – shopping in the morning was a good one, all you need now is another for the afternoon.'

'You make it sound simple, Horla.'

'It should be, for a clever Earthling like you.'

'I wish it was.'

'What do you normally do on a Saturday afternoon?'

'Not much, if Dad's not working we go for a ride somewhere in the car; he is working tomorrow, so we won't be doing that. Sometimes Mum and I join Grandma and Pip for a walk in the park, although Grandma stays at home mostly because she doesn't walk very well these days. That's about it really.'

'You go for a walk in the park,' Horla said thoughtfully, 'hmm, I wonder…'

'I've got it, Horla, I've got it!' Lucy then said, excitedly.

'What have you got?'

'A plan – listen to this: I reckon that Grandma will be so impressed with me going shopping alone tomorrow morning that she would give me permission to take Pip for a walk in the park in the afternoon if I asked her – what do you think?'

'Cor Lucy, that's what I was thinking, and why on Ivarnio didn't we think of it before?' Horla said in delight.

Lucy beamed and rubbed her hands together, saying, 'Yes, I'm sure she will, but I'll leave it till we come back from the shops tomorrow before I ask her.'

'Yes, good idea. My dad always says, if you take one step at a time, then things are less likely to go wrong.'

'You don't think anything *will* go wrong, do you Horla?'

'No, of course not, Lucy, we're going to have the best day ever.'

'Ooh, the best day ever,' Lucy grinned, 'I am so looking forward to that!'

11

THE GIRLS GO SHOPPING

The following morning, Lucy woke to the sound of Horla's voice.

'C'mon, sleepy-head, we've got a busy day ahead of us,' she said, peering from the mirror with a huge smile on her face.

'What time is it?' Lucy yawned back.

'Time to get up, that's what time it is.'

Lucy looked at her clock – it was eight o'clock. She shot up out of bed and, to Horla's surprise, she was fully clothed.

'Cracker-doo-doos, are you that poor that you can't afford pyjamas?' Horla laughed.

Lucy chuckled, 'It took me ages to get to sleep,

then I woke at about six and decided to get dressed; I must've nodded off again.'

'Just as well I woke you up then.'

'Yes, it is,' Lucy replied, putting on her shoes, 'although I'm surprised Mum hasn't been in to wake me. I'll go down and have my breakfast and come back in about fifteen minutes for you, OK?'

'OK, I'll do the same, see you then.'

Both girls gave each other the thumbs up and, after Horla disappeared from the mirror, Lucy made her way downstairs. Getting to the kitchen, she was surprised to find it empty, although the table had been laid, and a bowl with her usual cereal was at her place with a jug of milk beside it. Then she made out the sound of her mum's voice coming from the sitting-room... and she sounded rather irritated. The door was closed so Lucy decided to make her way over to it and listen.

'I'm *so* annoyed with myself, Mum, for saying she could do the shopping by herself today, I just don't know what possessed me to agree... yes, yes, I know she's in the juniors... yes, I know I used to go shopping for you at her age... yes, it's just that... OK, OK, Mum, I'll let her go, but promise you'll ring me if she doesn't arrive at your house by half-past nine, OK?... Yes, Mum... OK, Mum... yes, Mum, I'll stop worrying... OK, speak to you later, bye... bye.'

Lucy hurried back to her seat and was pouring the milk over her cereal when her worried-looking mum walked in.

'Morning, Mum,' she said to her cheerfully.

'Good morning, Lucy,' her mum replied with a sigh.

'I'm really looking forward to going shopping by myself today, Mum,' Lucy then said, enthusiastically, 'and I'll probably meet Emma shopping by herself too.'

'Are you certain she goes shopping by herself?'

'Yes, Mum… well she says she does anyway.'

Mum then gave her a worried look and said, 'Now are you *sure* you want to go on your own, I'm quite happy to go with you, you know!'

'Yes, I'm sure, Mum, and no, I don't want you to come with me – I can do it by myself, honestly; you relax and get on with something else.'

'You keep saying that…'

'And I mean it, Mum. It will help you get ahead of things and when I get back you'll be able to put your feet up like Dad does and have a read of the paper.'

Her mum stayed silent, but noticed Lucy looking at the clock; Lucy knew Horla would soon be waiting and needed to get out quick before her mum changed her mind completely.

'Don't rush your breakfast, Lucy,' Mum said to her, 'there's no urgency to get to the shops.'

'There is, Mum, I don't want anything to be sold out.'

'Oh, they won't sell out.'

'They might do,' Lucy said, finishing the last spoonful. Before her mum could argue back, she got up from her chair and ran upstairs saying, 'I'll be back in a tick – have the money ready please.'

***

As soon as Lucy's bedroom door closed, Horla appeared in the mirror saying, 'That was good timing, are you ready to go?'

'Yes, and quickly,' Lucy said to her, 'I think your persuading tactics are wearing off – we need to get out the house now before Mum changes her mind completely.'

'Oh no, Dad said that could happen – do I need to do it again?'

'I'm not sure, I've been doing my own persuading and it's just about still working; if we get out quick enough, we should be alright.'

'OK, take everything off the dressing table, I'm coming through.'

Lucy did as she was told, then stood back… she knew what was coming this time.

Schlluuuuuuppppp went the low sucking noise as Horla's distorted face vanished from the mirror. Seconds later, everything that had been on the dressing table floated back to where it came from, much to Lucy's delight.

'Come on, let's get going,' she said, walking towards the door.

'OK,' Horla replied, and then said, *'No,* I've told you before, *not you two!'*

Lucy gave a knowing laugh, and turned to see Fred and Ollie returning to their usual positions.

'You're definitely nuts,' she said, bumping into Horla as they tried to go through the doorway at the same time.

'Yes, I know; we're so alike aren't we?' Horla replied with a giggle.

'Shush, stop giggling, Mum will hear you.'

'OK, Boss,' Horla said, tickling Lucy in the ribs. Lucy resisted the temptation to tickle her back realising that, as she couldn't see her, she'd have probably missed anyway.

***

'There was a lot of giggling going on up there, what was so funny?' said her mum with a puzzled look on her face as Lucy came down the stairs.

'I was reading that joke book I got from the library, it's very funny,' said Lucy, telling a little white lie, and adding, 'I'm ready to go now so can I have the money please?'

'OK, here it is, and here's a bag and the list of

things you are getting; I'm sure you will remember everything, but, just in case, take it with you, *and please be careful crossing the roads.'*

'Of course I will, Mum, stop worrying,' Lucy replied, before hastily walking to the door and opening it wide. Horla stepped outside without a sound while Lucy turned and said, 'Bye Mum, see you later.' Her mum waved then watched anxiously as Lucy walked down the path, shutting the gate behind her.

'Your mum really does look worried,' Horla whispered.

'She is, I heard her talking on the phone to Grandma about it; goodness knows why she's making such a fuss, I mean, I'm only going to the shops. It wouldn't surprise me if she phones Grandma again fretting about it.'

'Shall we listen in and see if she does?'

'What? How can we do that?'

'Stop for a moment; I'm going to put my ear next to yours and then I'm going to concentrate.'

Lucy did as she was told, then listened in amazement to a conversation that was going on in her house.

'Hi, Mum, she's just left, striding down the road like a confident young lady I might add.'

Grandma chuckled and replied, 'OK, Louise, I'll expect her shortly, and I'll ring you as she leaves here; I don't know what you're worrying about though, I'm sure she's going to be just fine.'

'I hope you're right, but do you know something, it's not only because she's going out alone for the first time that I'm worried about her, but also because ever since Eleanor left I've heard her talking to herself.'

'Oh, don't concern yourself about that; yes she'll be missing Eleanor, but she's probably just thinking out loud that's all – I do it all the time, lots of people do.'

'Do they?'

'Yes, so relax – I'll speak to you later.'

'OK, I'll wait for your call, bye.'

'Right,' Lucy heard her mum say to herself putting down the phone, 'I'll just make myself a nice cup of tea to calm my nerves.'

Lucy was astonished, not so much for what was said in the conversation, but for the fact that she had heard the conversation at all.

'How the heck did you do that, Horla?' she said as they carried on walking.

'Easy, I just turn an ear in the direction I want to listen to then really concentrate; the fact that your ear touched mine meant that you could hear what was said too.'

'Wow, that's amazing!'

'Well I don't know about that, but now we know that your mum *is* worried about you.'

'Oh Mum's a fuss-pot: she worries when I do anything new.'

'Probably because you're an only child, I get that with my mum too,' Horla said.

'Do you?'

'Yes, mine even walks behind me when I'm on the monkey-bars to catch me if I fall; it is *sooo* embarrassing.'

'Oh, that *is* embarrassing.'

'Not as embarrassing as talking to yourself though.'

'Ha ha, if Mum only knew…'

'She thinks it's because you're missing Eleanor… are you?'

'Yes I am… I mean, it's great having you as my new friend, and I'm so glad you came, but… oh I do wish you could meet her.'

'Well I have *sort* of met her.'

'No, you only *saw* her, I mean *properly* meet her… and maybe even talk to her – you'd like her, I know you would.'

'I'm sure you're right and we will meet her, remember, I said I could help you see her.'

Lucy's heart raced with excitement at the thought; Horla was her *secret friend*, but maybe she should share her with Eleanor, who was, after all, her *best* friend. She was mulling this over in her head when suddenly, slowing down, she uttered, 'Uh oh!'

'What's up?' Horla replied.

Lucy nodded in the direction of a boy up ahead washing his dad's car.

'That's Harry from my class, he's very funny and always larking around, but sometimes he overdoes it and gets into trouble; he's soaked quite a few people from our class so I'm unlikely to get past without him turning that hosepipe on me; let's go another way.'

'No,' said Horla, 'don't worry, you'll be OK.'

The girls carried on and, as they got closer, Harry spotted Lucy, and an impish glint came in his eyes. He smiled an innocent smile and said, 'Hi, Lucy,' almost enticing her to come closer. Then suddenly, he aimed the hose up in the air so that the water would come down on Lucy's head, but instead of it going over Lucy, it rose higher and higher over Harry. With a puzzled look on his face, he then aimed it directly at Lucy, but still the water went straight up. Suddenly a shout came from the front of the house as Harry's dad came into view.

'Harry, what *do* you think you are playing at?' he said. Then without warning, all the water that had gone up came down like a cloudburst, soaking Harry and his dad to their skins. Harry's dad was furious.

'That's it, you're grounded, get in the house now!' he roared.

Sheepishly, Harry walked into the house, glancing back with embarrassment as he went. His dad, having realised what his son's intention had been, apologised to Lucy as she walked past, unaware that although one girl walked through the puddle, two sets of footprints came out the other side.

'That was a bit mean,' Lucy whispered, feeling just a little bit sorry for Harry at that moment.

Horla gave a fiendish laugh and replied, 'Yes, I know – funny though, wasn't it?'

'Yes it was,' Lucy answered, and after checking people weren't looking said, *'high five!'*

'High five!' Horla replied, slapping Lucy's hand.

Lucy chuckled, 'For a second there, I thought you might not know what a high five is.'

'I didn't until Dad explained it to me. He does it with Tristan. Now he greets Grandad with high fives. "Yo, Malcolm, high five!" he says, and now Grandad has all of his friends at the bowling club doing it. Mum won't though; she just raises her eyebrows and shakes her head because she thinks it's silly.'

'At least your grandad is doing it – my grandma gave up after the first attempt because she missed my hand and hit me on the nose.'

'Ooh, painful.'

'Yes it was. Anyway, better stop talking now, the shop's just round this corner.'

***

As they arrived at the bread shop, the baker, whose name was actually Mr. Baker, was in his usual friendly mood. He was a roly-poly sort of man, with rosy red cheeks, big ears, a long droopy moustache, and glasses perched on the end of his nose; he wore an apron with pictures of delicious-looking cakes on it, and a baker's hat with a windmill on top that turned as he moved, something he'd added himself to amuse children.

'Hello, Lucy,' he said. 'Are you on your own? Is your mum ill?'

'No, Mr. Baker, I volunteered to come by myself today,' Lucy replied, handing him the list.

'Oh that'll be a great help to her I'm sure,' he answered.

Lucy was looking up at him when her eyes nearly popped out of her head. As he read the list, she noticed the ends of his moustache starting to move; upwards and round and round they went until they finished up in a wonderful curl either side of his nose, making him look more like a circus ringmaster than a baker. Lucy was biting her lip, trying her best not to laugh, when the windmill on his hat started to turn. Faster and faster and faster again it went.

'Where on earth's that draught coming from?' Mr. Baker said, with a puzzled look on his face. He then glanced up just in time to see his hat suddenly lift off his head and start flying around the shop.

'*Oh my word!*' he said, watching as it did a loop-the-loop and disappeared out of the doorway. He turned open-mouthed to Lucy in disbelief and, stutteringly, exclaimed, 'Did... did, you see th-th-that; my hat's just flown out of the door!'

But unbeknown to him, while he was saying those few words, his hat flew back faster than the eye could see and landed back on his head without him realising.

'But it's on your head, Mr. Baker,' Lucy replied.

Mr. Baker, shocked, put his hands to his head.

'Oh my word, so it is, my imagination must be playing tricks on me – hat flying out of the door indeed, whatever will I think of next,' he said, shaking his head.

He then set about filling Lucy's bag with things from the list, finally coming to the last items which were two gingerbread men, Lucy's favourite. As he was about to pick them up, Mr. Baker suddenly jerked his hand back as if it had been bitten by a rattlesnake.

'*Arrrggghhh!*' he squawked in shock as the two gingerbread men sprung to life and started fighting with each other. He stood open-mouthed once more as they sparred like professional boxers, bobbing and weaving, trying to hit each other, until, finally, they did – at the same time – and knocked each other's heads off!

'Oh dear, I really must get to bed earlier, yes, that's it – a bit more beauty sleep is what I need. Getting up so early to bake bread is not good for my brain I'm sure,' he muttered to himself, convinced he was hallucinating. Then picking up two whole gingerbread men he said, 'There we are, Lucy, order complete.'

'Thank you, Mr. Baker,' Lucy replied, handing him the money. As she received the change, she asked, 'Could I now have two extra gingerbread men in a separate bag please? I'll pay for them from my pocket money.'

Mr. Baker, still a little confused after his experience, picked up the "boxers" and said, 'You can have these two for free, providing you don't mind their heads being broken off; goodness knows how that happened, I must have got the mixture a little wrong, but I'm sure they will taste just the same.'

'Thank you very much, Mr. Baker,' Lucy replied, taking the bag from him.

After saying goodbye, she turned to leave, but not before a lady walked in, and, spotting his moustache, said, 'Oh my word, Mr. Baker, you do look rather handsome today.'

'Oh thank you,' he replied, his rosy red cheeks going a little redder, and wondering what on earth had made her say that. *After all*, he thought, *I don't look any different today than I do any other day!*

***

'That was so funny,' said Lucy, as they walked across to the newsagents. 'Poor Mr. Baker, he looked so confused at what was happening, and he'll get a big surprise when he looks in the mirror later.'

'When I saw him with that big moustache I couldn't resist it,' giggled Horla, 'and from the sound of it, that lady who came in couldn't resist it either!'

'Oh yes, she really liked Mr. Baker's new look.'

'She'll probably ask him to marry her.'

'Yes, I suppose so… oh hang on, Horla.'

'What is it?'

'See that boy with the brown jacket on, that's "Bob the Rob" from our class who I told you about, and it looks like he's going in to the newsagent's too.'

'Ah ha, so that's Bob the Rob. Well if your suspicions are right, he won't be able to control himself in a shop like that; come on, let's see what he gets up to.'

As they entered the shop, Horla, whose curiosity was really aroused, followed him, while Lucy went to get the papers. He made his way over to the sweet shelves and casually looked around to see if he was being watched, which he was, although of course he didn't know it. Satisfied nobody was looking his way, he put something in each of his three pockets, then picked the paper and magazine he had been sent out to get and placed them on the counter. As he passed over a £5 note to pay, the newsagent, Mr. Page, said to him, 'Will that be all?' which was something he said to all of his customers as they came to pay.

'Yeah,' Bob the Rob lied in reply, obviously having no intention of paying for the things he had hidden.

Suddenly, a small squeaky voice came from his left pocket. *'Don't forget to pay for me,'* it said, and a Mars Bar came shooting out and landed on the counter. *'And me,'* said another squeaky voice, this time coming from his right pocket as a packet of Chocolate Buttons shot out and landed on the counter. *'And what about me,'* said another squeaky voice from his top pocket as a Curly Wurly popped out and landed by the other sweets.

Mr. Page, who'd seen a lot of strange things in his time, said, 'That was a very good trick, I don't know how you did it but that will be £4.80,' and proceeded to hand over the change. A look of horror came on Bob the Rob's face; he was completely shocked by what had happened and even more shocked at the thought of having to explain to his parents why he only had 20p change out of £5. He did look a sorry sight as he left the shop. Lucy, who was approaching the counter when all this happened, was greeted by Mr. Page.

'Hello, Lucy,' he said. 'Good trick that boy did just then; are you a magician as well and have made your mum disappear?'

'No, Mr. Page,' Lucy smiled. 'I don't do tricks; I've come by myself this morning.'

As she said this, her two plaits turned upwards and started waving at the newsagent.

'Good grief, you're all at it,' Mr. Page said with a huge grin on his face. 'I expect you'll be pulling rabbits out of your shopping bag next.'

Lucy, realising what had just happened, couldn't help but laugh. She paid for the papers and left the shop, leaving Mr. Page shaking his head and wondering how she and the boy had done the tricks he'd just witnessed.

'So, your suspicions were right, Lucy,' Horla said once outside. 'You and your classmates were quite justified in calling him "Bob the Rob" – he needs to be watched extra closely from now on.'

'Yes, you're right, and I'll tell everyone how he tried to steal this morning, although I'll not mention anything about the talking sweets.'

'No, you'd better not…they'd think you were loopy if you did.'

'Yes, that's what I'm afraid of.'

'"Loopy Lucy"… hey, that suits you!'

'Watch it, mate!'

'I was only saying…'

'Shut yer cake-hole and take the two gingerbread men off the top of the shopping bag while nobody's looking.'

'I've got them.'

'OK, now let's get to Grandma's house before Mum starts worrying even more.'

12

HORLA
MEETS PIP

As they reached Grandma's house, Lucy was delighted to see Pip, Grandma's little dog, looking out of the window. As soon as he saw Lucy he started barking excitedly and ran to the front door. When the door was opened, he ran out and jumped up at Lucy as he always did, his tail wagging like a car windscreen wiper in a downpour.

With his front paws on her legs, Lucy bent down and stroked him. As she bent down even lower, he licked her face as he always did because he was so pleased to see her, but then he walked away from Lucy and started sniffing. Lucy was suddenly horrified as she realised that although Pip couldn't

see Horla, his sense of smell was so powerful, he knew she was there. Lucy was about to take hold of his collar when the strangest thing happened: Pip stood up on his back legs and, with his front legs in the air, apparently leaning against nothing, started wagging his tail even faster and began licking fresh air.

'Good grief, that's weird,' Grandma said. 'You haven't brought along that imaginary friend you had when you were little have you?' she continued, laughing out loud at her joke.

'No, Grandma, don't be silly, Pip's just imagining Mum's with me as usual and pretending to give her a lick as well.'

'Hmm, that's even weirder,' Grandma replied, before turning and walking back into the house saying, 'Come on in then and we'll have our refreshments,' as she went. Lucy followed, and so did Horla, who was very careful not to get in the way.

After the drinks were poured, Lucy and her grandma settled in the sitting room to have their usual Saturday morning treat. Normally, Pip would lie down at Lucy's feet, but at that moment he was happy to stay in the kitchen where, before his very eyes, something very unusual was taking place.

A paper bag suddenly appeared in mid-air, and from it came a headless gingerbread man. A second later, it was not only minus its head, but also a leg, as it broke off and flew through the air in his direction. He caught it expertly in his mouth and quickly devoured it, then watched as the rest of it disappeared in mouth-sized chunks above him. Looking hungrily for more, he was delighted when another headless gingerbread man appeared and the procedure was repeated.

'Go and see what that little rascal is up to, Lucy,' Grandma said on hearing Pip moving about in the kitchen.

Lucy did as she was told and arrived just in time to see the two gingerbread men's heads, both with big smiles on their faces, appearing from a floating paper bag, then quickly disappearing, one into Pip's mouth, and one into thin air! Lucy, without thinking, clapped her hands at this strange but amusing sight.

'What's he doing?' shouted Grandma from the living room.

'Oh, hmm, he thinks he's a cat, Grandma – he's got his head inside a paper bag,' which he did have, doggedly trying to scoff every last crumb available.

'Well that hardly deserves a round of applause, so don't encourage him; he's barmy enough as it is!'

Just then the phone rang. On hearing her grandma in conversation, Lucy whispered to Horla, 'Well, *that* was unusual!'

'*Unusual?* Have you not seen someone giving a dog a biscuit before?'

'No, I've *never* "not seen" someone giving a dog a biscuit before!'

Horla held back a laugh as Pip's ears pricked up at the mention of the word biscuit. Then Lucy explained to her, 'The animal rescue centre told us that because he's white with brown markings, he was called "Biscuit" by the horrible people who used to own him. "Do you want a biscuit, Biscuit?" they would tease, then *not* give him a biscuit. They thought that was funny,' she fumed.

'Idiots!'

'Exactly!'

Lucy was still nodding her head when Grandma shouted, 'Lucy, your mum would like a word with you.'

'OK, coming.'

'Guess what,' her mum said when she picked up the phone, 'I've just had a chat with Sam. Eleanor wanted to speak to you so I said if she called back in about half an hour you'd be in by then.'

'Oh that's great. OK, Mum, we'll be home shortly, oh I mean *I'll* be home shortly,' Lucy said, going a bit red in the face as she realised she'd nearly slipped up.

Her grandma laughed out loud at her mistake, joking, 'So you really have brought your imaginary friend along with you!'

Horla silently came into the room on hearing this and, looking around, her attention was drawn to photographs on a bookcase next to a rocking chair. One in particular caught her eye: it was a photograph of Lucy holding a small teddy bear dressed in tartan, and it had a tiny red scarf around its neck. She quietly walked over to get a closer look and, unable to believe her eyes, she gasped.

Grandma looked at Lucy, and said, 'What's up?'

Thinking quickly, Lucy pointed to the rocking chair and in pretend shock said, 'Look, it's my imaginary friend, she's sitting in the rocking chair!'

Grandma shook her head and laughed at her granddaughter's witty reply. Pip, meanwhile, having finished off the crumbs, came in and started sniffing around Horla's feet. Lucy realising, called him to her then said, 'Right, Grandma, I'd better get home to take my call.'

'OK,' she replied, getting up slowly from her chair.

Seeing Grandma's back turned, Horla couldn't resist the urge to give the chair a quick rock before she left. To her horror, the rocking chair not only rocked, it creaked as well. Now it was Grandma's turn to gasp. Lucy hadn't moved the chair, she knew that, she was standing next to her, and it wasn't Lucy's imaginary friend – that was just a joke, but the chair moved, yes it definitely moved, she'd heard it creak; yes, she'd definitely heard it creak.

Nervously, and to Lucy's astonishment, she whispered, 'Is that you, Freddie?'

Lucy looked at her grandma open-mouthed, and a shiver went down her spine; she'd assumed Horla had made the chair move, not her grandad who'd died before she was born. Grandma turned to her and in a sad voice said, 'I hear the chair creaking sometimes when I'm in bed at night; I feel as if he's still here, in the house.' She went forward to the chair and rubbed her hand over the cushion, then the seat, saying, 'This was his favourite chair, you know; he'd often fall asleep in it, snore right through *EastEnders* he would.'

At that moment Lucy felt so sad for Grandma – she obviously missed her husband terribly. Pip, on the other hand, started rolling about on the floor, mouth wide open, as if in hysterics at her remarks.

'Well I'm glad you think it's funny, you little rascal,' Grandma said, suddenly sounding cheerful again.

'But you don't *really* think he's here do you, Grandma, I mean, he didn't answer you did he?'

'No, but then he never did listen, the daft old beggar,' she replied, roaring with laughter.

Lucy nervously laughed along with her; she was sure she'd have loved her grandad, but she wasn't so keen on meeting his ghost! Composing herself she said, 'Right, I really must be off for Eleanor's call now, Grandma.'

'OK,' Grandma replied, giving her a hug. 'Be very careful of the traffic.'

'Don't worry, I will,' Lucy replied as she picked up the shopping and made her way to the door. As she opened it, she felt Horla squeezing past her, quickly followed by Pip, who was immediately called back and told off by Grandma.

'You know very well you do *not* leave this house without your lead on,' she scolded as Pip came running back with his tail between his legs.

"Best to do as I'm told, he chuckled to himself, *otherwise there'll be no biscuits for Biscuit tonight!"*

13

THE DISAPPEARANCE
OF TARTAN TED
REVEALED

Lucy looked back and gave one last wave to Grandma.
As soon as she was out of earshot, she said, 'Horla,
tell me it was *you* who moved the rocking chair.'

'No, I didn't move it,' Horla replied matter-of-
factly.

'Oh my God – Grandad's come back to haunt
us!'

'Relax, I'm only joking – it was me; I wasn't
expecting it to creak like it did though.'

'And I wasn't expecting Grandma to talk to it –
that freaked me out that did.'

'Yes, that *was* odd, and the bit about hearing it creaking at night was strange, but do you know what was stranger still?'

'What?'

'Pip's behaviour when she said it.'

'Oh come off it, he's just a dog, he wouldn't understand what Grandma was on about.'

'I wouldn't be too sure.'

'*Pffft!*'

'I'm just saying…'

'Anyway, what on earth made you gasp like that?'

'It was that photograph, the one of you holding the tartan teddy bear with a red scarf around its neck.'

'Oh, that one – but why did it make you gasp?'

'Well, it's just that… well, do you know where that teddy bear is now?'

'No, I haven't a clue. It disappeared one day and hasn't been seen since. I was only a toddler at the time, so it was my mum who told me later of it doing, what she called, "a vanishing act". She was upset at the time because it had been her teddy when she was little and apparently, when I was asked where it was, I just kept pointing at the mirror.'

'Oh Lucy, I can hardly believe it, but I think I've got a confession to make. When *I* was a toddler, I went missing; people searched for hours, they even called the police to search for me. Then I just turned up in my bedroom, which had been searched along with the rest of the house earlier. My parents heard movement in my bedroom, rushed upstairs and there I was, sitting on the floor… holding a tartan teddy bear, with a red scarf around his neck!'

It was Lucy's turn to gasp, but Horla continued, 'It was at that point that Dad had to confess to Mum about his powers and insisted that I be kept away from the mirrors because I may have inherited those powers.'

'Gosh, that means that my imaginary friend wasn't so imaginary after all – it was you all along!'

'So here we are thinking that we've only known each other for a few days, when in fact we've known each other for years,' Horla chuckled.

'Not that either of us can remember much about it,' Lucy replied.

'No, that's true – although I vaguely remembered your room, don't you remember I told you everything seemed familiar when I saw it?'

'Oh yes, that's right.'

'And the reason why, was because I'd been in it before.'

'Wow, isn't that incredible… but I thought when you looked in your mirror you had to concentrate to find me; do you think that's what you did as a toddler?'

'I must have done, being alone in my room I must have wished I had someone to play with – and being here before was probably the reason I was able to find you so easily this time.'

'That's amazing; you know, I think what's happened was destined to happen and that we were meant to be friends.'

'Maybe, but even if we weren't, we are now!' Horla replied, squeezing Lucy's hand.

Lucy squeezed Horla's hand back saying, 'And don't forget about Pip, he's your friend now too.'

'Oh I couldn't forget Pip, he's adorable!'

'And what about the tartan teddy; do you still have it?'

'No, Mum passed it on to Vespa, that's her friend June's baby girl – she got hold of it one day when they were visiting and wouldn't let go; howled the place down when June tried to hand it back. So Mum said to me, "You've finished with this, haven't you Horla?" Well I hadn't really, but I felt as though I had to say yes.'

'Oh my mum's like that too, always wanting to get rid of *my* stuff before I've finished with it, and yet she's got two *massive* wardrobes full of *her* stuff.'

'Mine has too, *and* her own shoe rack.'

'Oh well, never mind, it's nice to know a fourth person is having the pleasure of owning it.'

'Yes, that's true.'

'Did you give it a name?'

'Yes, I called it "China Ted" because it said "Made in China" on the label, although nobody had a clue where that was, apart from Dad of course, but he didn't let on. What did *you* call it?'

'Well Mum just called it Tartan Ted, apparently, but I didn't get a chance to give it a name because it was *stolen* from me before I could make up my mind.'

'Whoops, sorry about that.'

'No worries – anyway, best stop talking now, we're nearly home and I don't want the neighbours to think I'm loopy.'

'I expect they already know.'

'Hey, watch it!'

'Only kidding!'

'Just as well – now stop talking!'

'OK, Captain, message understood – temporary closure of gob about to be actioned!'

***

Within minutes they were approaching Lucy's house.

'Right,' she said, trying her best to talk without moving her lips, 'you walk quietly in behind me, sneak up to my bedroom and I'll join you as soon as Eleanor phones; I'll bring the phone up with me and you can listen in to the conversation.'

'OK,' Horla whispered back.

'I'm home!' shouted Lucy as she walked in through the back door into the kitchen.

'Hi, darling,' replied her relieved mum as she came to greet her. 'Did you get everything?'

'Yes, Mum, everything that was on the list; I haven't missed Eleanor's call have I?'

'No, she's due to call any min— oh, that must be her now!'

'I'll get it, and I'll go to my room and lie on the bed talking to her, OK?'

'Oh, OK.'

Lucy was so excited, she rushed to the phone, grabbed it and raced upstairs trying her best to breathe and talk at the same time. In her room, she put it on speaker and asked the question she'd been dying to ask.

'So come on, Elle – tell me what your new school is like.'

'Oh, Lucy, I wish we hadn't moved,' Eleanor replied sadly.

'Why?' Lucy asked, surprised.

'Because I don't like it, in fact I hate it.'

'But why, why do you hate it?'

'Well, I haven't made any friends yet, that's why.'

'But, Elle, you're so popular; I thought you would easily make friends.'

'Well I haven't, I mean, there's no one nasty like the Taylors or anything like that, it's just that they never invite me to join in with any of their games.'

'That's a bit mean – why won't they?'

Lucy could hear the frustration in Eleanor's voice as she replied, 'Well at first it was because they have their own sets of friends and didn't even seem to notice me.'

'Now that's not on,' Lucy replied sympathetically.

Eleanor then gave a massive sigh and said, 'And it's also...'

'It's also what? Come on, out with it.'

'Well I was in the playground, hoping to be noticed, when suddenly, your flippin' joke about the spider crawling out of my pocket came true!'

'What? You mean that did actually happen?' Lucy said in amazement.

'Yes,' Eleanor said in an annoyed voice, 'and I'm furious with my dad because he said he'd got rid of it.'

Lucy tried not to laugh at what sounded like a very funny scene and said, sympathetically, 'So what happened then?'

'Well I was close to a group of my class-mates and just when I thought they had noticed me and maybe were going to invite me to play with them, they suddenly screamed and ran away from me shouting, "*Spider spider!*" I looked down and there it was, looking out from my cardigan pocket as if it was my best mate.'

At this point Lucy couldn't help herself and burst out laughing.

'*It's not funny!*' Eleanor shouted, 'They're now calling me "Spider Girl" and running away every time I go near them.'

'Oh, right,' Lucy said, becoming serious again. 'So what happened to the spider?'

'Oh well, you know me, I'm not scared of spiders, so I thought, if they're being silly, then I'll be silly, so I picked it up and ran after them with it.'

'Uh oh'.

'Yes I know, I shouldn't have done that; now they think it's funny to run away from me *whenever* I go near them. Oh I just wish I could do something to impress them, maybe then I would be accepted.'

Lucy, for once, was lost for words; she remembered how she had intended to finish the chess game with Eleanor on Skype – but she hadn't, she'd cleared the board and put it away. She felt bad about that. Then she felt even worse when Eleanor asked, 'Have *you* been feeling lonely without *me?*'

The guilt rushed through Lucy's body because the fact was that since Horla had arrived, she hadn't felt lonely at all.

'Yes, I have,' she replied.

'Then please, please come and visit me soon, *I'm really missing you.*'

Lucy could tell that Eleanor was close to tears and made up her mind: she was going to nag and nag her parents until they gave in and took her to Liverpool. It was important – her best friend needed her and she didn't want to let her down!

14

THE DRESS, REVERSE PHYSICS AND THE BUBBLE

'You should go and visit her,' were Horla's words as soon as the call ended.

'Yes, I know, and I'm desperate to do that and I've already asked Mum but she says it's out of the question at the moment. It'll be a while yet before we can go all that way, and besides, we have to wait until we are invited, our family can't just turn up on their doorstep, can we?'

'No, I mean *us* go and visit her,' persisted Horla, 'we could go this afternoon, don't you remember, I said I could help you see her.'

Lucy was baffled. 'How could we get to see her and how could I go out without Mum realising I was gone?'

'Don't worry about how we get to see her, I'll explain that later, but remember your original plan for this afternoon was to take Pip out for a walk, if you can get permission we could go then.'

Lucy's eyes brightened. Although still unsure as to how they could possibly travel all that way and back without being missed, she decided to go downstairs and put the plan into action. As she entered the room, she found her mum now relaxing, reading the morning paper.

'Mum,' she said, walking up to her.

'Yes?' her mum replied, looking up from the paper.

'There's something I'd *really, really* like to do.'

'Ooh, this sounds important. What is it that you'd *really, really* like to do?'

'I'd like to take Pip to the park by myself – can I phone Grandma and see if it's OK?'

'Good grief Lucy, I am impressed, the shops this morning, the park this afternoon, all by yourself – where *has* all this confidence come from?'

'Don't be silly, Mum, I'm not a baby anymore, you know.'

Her mum laughed and said, 'OK, I tell you what, *I'll* ask Grandma for you, but while I do that, you go into the kitchen and butter four rounds of bread for sandwiches for lunch.'

Lucy was really pleased and said, 'Thanks, Mum, and don't forget to tell her it's something I'd *really, really like to do!*'

While Lucy went to the kitchen, her mum took a phone upstairs into a bedroom where she knew she wouldn't be heard and rang her own mum.

'Mum, you're never going to believe this, but Lucy's so full of confidence after her shopping trip earlier, she now wants to take Pip out to the park this afternoon, *by herself!*'

'*You're joking!*'

'No, I'm not – she says I'm to tell you it's something she *really, really* wants to do.'

'Oh dear, that sounds serious,' Grandma replied laughing. 'It's amazing what a little bit of confidence can do, isn't it?'

'Yes, you're right. What do you think we should do?' Mum asked.

'I'm not so sure really. I wouldn't want to damage this new-found confidence by saying no, but taking Pip to the park is a big responsibility.'

'Yes, I know.'

'On the other hand,' Grandma said, 'he does always come back when he's called and, when you think about it, when we all go to the park, you and I are often chatting away while she and Pip are playing without us being involved.'

'Yes, you're right there.'

'And it would absolutely make her day to take Pip out, wouldn't it?'

'Yes,' Mum replied, 'it would, and I must admit I'm a little bit less worried now that she's been out alone this morning... although I'll still worry.'

'Of course you will, it's only natural, but do you know what?'

'What?'

'I think we should let her do it.'

'Well... if *you're* happy for her to do it...'

'Yes, I am now, so let's stop dithering about it and tell her to come round, say, one o'clock.'

'Hmm, OK, Mum, I'll send her round for one o'clock.'

***

Lucy's mum went downstairs to give her daughter the good news. Smiling, she said, 'Grandma says it's OK for you to take Pip out this afternoon, and she's expecting you to call for him at one o'clock.'

Lucy's eyes lit up. 'Oh thanks, Mum,' she replied and, having finished her chore, made an excuse to go up to her bedroom, where, unbeknown to her, a bored Horla had been doing something Lucy just wasn't expecting.

'Horla, I've got permission, Grandma says I *can* take Pip to the park this afternoon,' she said excitedly, although not too loudly.

But instead of an immediate reply, there was a short silence followed by a muffled cry of, '*Tah dah!*' as the wardrobe door opened and a dress popped out – then twirled round like a supermodel in a fashion show.

Lucy laughed as Horla said, 'I couldn't resist it, it's such a lovely dress that I just *had* to see what it looked like on me; the only problem is, I can't see me in your mirror!'

'Well why don't you whizz back and have a look at yourself in *your* mirror then?'

'Ooh, that's a good idea,' Horla said, and immediately all the things on the dressing table lifted up, flew over, and landed on the bed, much to Lucy's delight.

'Right, hang on; I'll be back in a tick.'

Schlluuuuuupppppp, the low, creepy sucking sound went as the dress moved towards the mirror then disappeared, and, seconds later, Lucy watched with a smile on her face as Horla pranced around in front of her own mirror in the dress.

Lucy couldn't see why Horla liked it, because she hated it. It was so old-fashioned and very, very "girly", and, being a bit of a tomboy, she much preferred to wear trousers. Grandma had bought it in a charity shop and said the style was from the nineteen fifties – and Lucy wished it had stayed in the nineteen fifties!

'I thought you could wear it for a party,' she had said with a look of triumph on her face, 'it only cost me £2.'

'Oh thank you, Grandma,' Lucy had replied sounding grateful, but thinking, *I wouldn't be seen dead in this!*

The problem was that her grandma was old – much older than the twenty-one she claimed to be, so the dress would have been in fashion when she was a girl… and she obviously thought it still was!

Satisfied that it looked good on her, Horla said, 'Stand back, property of Planet Earth being returned.' *Schlluuuuuuppppp*, went the low, creepy sucking noise again as Horla's distorted face disappeared from the mirror and the dress reappeared in Lucy's bedroom.

'I hope you don't mind me trying this dress on, it's ever so pretty,' Horla then said.

'No, of course not,' Lucy replied, seemingly to a talking dress, 'but you know, there's something I don't understand.'

'What's that?'

'The way that dress and the tartan teddy can be seen in your world but anything from your world can't be seen here – *why is that?*'

'Well, Dad's friend Tristan, who's very clever, says it's because of "reverse physics".'

'Reverse physics, what the flippin' heck is that?'

'Well, he says that when we come into your world we move forward in time, and because we don't exist in your year yet, we can't be seen, but, anything coming the other way, because it's from the future, can be seen.'

'Oh, I see.'

'Do you?'

'Well, no, not really.'

'Neither do I, but Tristan's quite pleased it works that way.'

'Why?'

'Because he walks out in the middle of winter wearing a tee shirt pretending he's tough, when in fact he wears a big heavy overcoat that Dad gave him on top of it.'

'Oh that's a good trick.'

'It is, he's a bit of a joker, Tristan. Anyway, forget about him – you've got permission to take Pip to the park like you thought you would then?'

'Yes and Mum doesn't seem at all worried this time; I expect she'll relax and put her feet up like I suggested.'

'Oh that's good. Now, what we need is a picture of Eleanor; can we take that one of her on your bedside cabinet with us?'

'Yes, we can, but why do we need a picture of Eleanor?'

'Because I need to concentrate on what a person's face looks like to find them, but, if I don't know them very well, I take their photograph with me to look at on the journey, and then the bubble goes right to them wherever they are.'

'Bubble, what bubble?'

'The bubble we're going to travel to Liverpool in.'

'We're travelling in a bubble?' Lucy gasped in horror, 'But bubbles always burst!'

'This one doesn't, so stop worrying – you'll see what I'm talking about shortly. Now let me get out of this dress before I forget I'm wearing it and frighten the life out of people!'

15

THE VISIT TO LIVERPOOL

At one o'clock that afternoon, Lucy and Horla arrived at Grandma's house to collect Pip. This time Horla stayed well back so the dog wouldn't sense her and get excited in front of Grandma. Spotting Lucy from the window, he barked and ran to the front door to greet her, making Grandma realise that her granddaughter had arrived.

'Well, I didn't expect to see you again so soon,' she said, opening the door. 'Come on in while I get his lead for him.' Lucy stepped inside to an excited Jack Russell, who got even more excited on seeing the lead being taken off the hook in the hallway.

'Now are you sure you're going to be all right with him? If you want to change your mind, then that's OK by me.'

'No, Grandma, I don't want to change my mind, I *really, really* want to do this.'

'Yes, so I believe. In that case, pop this lead on the little rascal and away you go.'

Within a minute the lead was on and Lucy and Pip were walking out of the door.

'Bye then, Grandma, we'll see you later – and don't worry, we'll be fine,' Lucy said, with a wave of her hand. Her grandma waved back with a big smile on her face as Lucy and Pip set off for the park. As they disappeared from view she picked up the phone and called her daughter.

'Hi, Louise, they've just left,' she said.

'OK, Mum, you set off and I'll meet you at the park gates.'

'OK, see you there.'

Pip, meanwhile, was pulling on his lead as he realised he was heading to his favourite place; all those trees, all those smells really excited him. Lucy knew Horla was somewhere near but didn't know where exactly when, suddenly, approaching the park café, the dog's tail wagged furiously and he shot off, pulling Lucy with him.

At the back of the café, out of sight of everyone, Horla shouted, *'Over here!'* But she didn't have to as Pip knew exactly where she was and darted towards her. When they got together Horla said, 'Right, now it's important to do exactly as I say: pick Pip up, hold him tight and on my count of three, jump up into the air.'

'OK,' Lucy replied excitedly, not questioning this unusual instruction.

On the count of three, the two girls leapt into the air, where a strange thing happened. Instead of coming back down to the ground as you would expect, they continued to rise. Lucy's mouth was wide open in astonishment as she realised they were in a bluey-grey transparent bubble that was going higher and higher. Even more astonishing was the fact that, once inside the bubble, Horla had become visible! Just like in the mirror – *Lucy could really see her!*

As it rose above the café, Lucy spotted her grandma and her mum who'd decided at the last minute to follow and keep an eye on her. They'd kept at a discreet distance and were now scratching their heads wondering how on earth a little girl and a dog could disappear into thin air.

'Don't worry, they can't see us,' said Horla, who had realised Lucy was looking in their direction. 'If we get a move on we'll be back before they get too worried; take out that photo of Eleanor and let's get going.'

'But I don't think we'll have the time, don't you realise, I thought they trusted me but obviously they don't and they've followed to check on me.'

'Hmm, you're probably right, so in that case I'll make them forget why they've come to the park.'

'How long could you make them forget for though? Remember your persuasion tactic started to wear off on Mum.'

'Yes, I know. That's because adults have bigger brains than children and so I need to concentrate even more to overcome *their* thoughts. But don't worry, I'll check it's working as we go along, although I'll need to be in two places at once, which I've never tried before, but I'm sure I can do it.'

'What do you mean, be in two places at once?'

'I'll tell you about it as we go along, but first of all I need to really concentrate.'

That was Lucy's cue to keep quiet and not say a word: she just looked on as the bubble hovered above her relatives, and Horla stared intently at them. Finally, her mum and grandma, seemingly without a care in the world, set off at a leisurely pace towards the park lake. Horla then said, 'Right, let's have that photo and we'll be on our way.'

As soon as she looked at the photograph, the bubble started to move. It rose higher and higher, until, once above the trees, it started to speed forwards in the direction of Liverpool. Faster and faster it went, going faster than the fastest cars on the motorway below, going faster even than the express train heading for Scotland. And yet inside, there was no feeling of speed, no movement to bring on travel

sickness, no noises to distract the travellers from their thoughts, just a calmness that made travelling this way an awe-inspiring experience.

Lucy was dumbstruck and hardly said a word throughout the journey, staring instead at the scenes below, and finding it hard to believe what was happening. Horla looked at her, recalling how she herself was bowled over on *her* first journey in the bubble when Tristan asked for her dad's help after he'd missed a flight. It had been a wonderful experience, especially catching up and flying alongside the plane as it flew over the sea to Ireland, with Tristan's work colleague sitting at a window seat, unaware that Tristan was just a few metres away. She wasn't surprised that Lucy was so quiet, but broke the silence by saying, 'Right, now remember I said I'll need to be in two places at once?'

'Oh yes,' Lucy replied, coming back to "reality".

'Well at this moment, as you know, your mum and grandma have forgotten about you coming to the park, and the plan is to keep them forgetting until they get back home.'

'OK...'

'So I'll be disappearing from time to time to keep them forgetting, and of course, busy, as the longer they are out, the better.'

'What, you're leaving me up here alone?'

'Don't worry, it'll only be for a few minutes at a time, and anyway, you're not alone, you've got your "guard dog" with you.'

Lucy smiled and looked at Pip, who stood up and stuck out his chest as if he understood exactly what had just been said.

'There we are, now how could anyone be worried with that sort of protection? Now, I won't be a moment, I'll just see how they are getting on.'

Lucy watched as Horla disappeared, *well almost* disappeared: to her eyes it was like what she imagined seeing a ghost would be like, a bit like Nearly Headless Nick in the *Harry Potter* films. Pip cocked his head to one side, bemused, as Horla's "ghost" stood motionless in deep concentration.

A few minutes later, Horla was back to her normal self and said, 'Lucy, is your mum afraid of water?'

'No, my mum is a good swimmer, why do you ask?'

'I'll tell you later, back in a tick.'

That was a strange question, Lucy thought, as Horla returned to being as visible as Nearly Headless Nick again. As before, she was back to being herself within minutes, a procedure that was repeated a number of times on the journey, much to Horla's annoyance though, as being in two places at once was proving to be more difficult than she had imagined it would be.

Eventually, Lucy spotted the famous Liver Birds coming into view.

'Look,' she said, pointing, 'I've seen those on television; we've arrived, we're in Liverpool!'

The bubble started to slow down. Over the Albert Dock it went, past the two cathedrals and onwards in the direction of Sefton Park, the prettiest park in Liverpool. As it got to the park, it hovered over a crowd of children standing by some very tall trees at the side of the lake. As Lucy took a closer look, there, standing back from the crowd, on her own and looking a little forlorn, was Eleanor. Pip spotted her too and he barked and wagged his tail. Horla got the bubble to move in closer and both girls soon realised why the crowd had gathered: up at the top of an extremely tall tree was a cat, which, they found out, belonged to a girl named Emily.

'He's been up there a long time and seems too frightened to make his way back down,' they overheard Emily say to her friends. 'I've called the fire brigade but there's nobody available because they're all too busy trying to put out a very big fire somewhere.'

Tears were starting to form in her eyes; she obviously loved her cat and was desperately worried it might fall out of the tree.

'Do you think those children are from Eleanor's school?' Horla said, surveying the scene.

'Possibly, and they might also be the ones she wants to impress,' Lucy replied.

'Hmm, if that were the case, this could be the perfect situation to impress them.'

'I don't follow?'

'Well, if Eleanor were to climb up the tree and save the cat, who would not be impressed?'

'Ooh, I'm not so sure, Horla – she's a good climber but I don't think she could do that!'

'She could with my help.'

'Horla, you'd need to make her as agile as Mowgli in *Jungle Book* for her to climb *that* tree.'

'I don't know who Mowgli in *Jungle Book* is, but if it's a girl who climbs trees without fear, then yes, I can do that.'

'It's a boy, actually, but yes, he does climb trees without fear.'

'Well then, shall we show everyone that we girls are as good as boys at climbing trees?'

Lucy gave a nervous giggle and then replied enthusiastically, 'Yes, let's do that, but please, be careful – I wouldn't want her to fall and hurt herself.'

'Don't worry, she won't,' Horla replied, 'but let me concentrate on the cat first.'

Lucy then watched as the cat suddenly stood up on the branch, then it sat back down again, then it stood up a second time, and sat back down for a second time.

'OK, I'm happy with that,' Horla said, 'it does as it is told, now let's put the plan into action, or rather, you put the plan into action.'

'Me?'

'Yes, you – she's your best friend isn't she?'

'Yes but…'

'Well just go and tell her to rescue the cat.'

'But…'

'No buts; this is a great opportunity to help Eleanor, so get a move on before the cat falls out of the tree.'

Lucy realised Horla was right; it was now or never. As soon as the bubble touched down, she raced off towards Eleanor. Approaching her from behind, she put her hands round Eleanor's head and covered her eyes, saying, 'Guess who this is!'

'*Lucy!*' Eleanor cried, turning round in disbelief, 'But… I've just spoken to you… how come you're here, I mean, how… how did you get here so quickly?'

'No time to explain Elle, I've just come to say a quick hello because you sounded so sad on the phone, not having any friends and all that – no one knows I'm here so don't you breathe a word about it to your parents.'

Eleanor looked across to the group of girls as Lucy said that.

'I won't say anything,' she replied, staring intently at them.

'Are they the girls you'd like to be friends with?' Lucy asked.

'Yes,' Eleanor replied, sadly, 'some of them are.'

'Well then, you wanted to impress them, so now's your big chance.'

'Huh?'

'Go and rescue the cat, silly; you know you're a good climber.'

As Lucy said that, an enormous feeling of self-confidence swept through Eleanor's body. She straightened herself up and, with a huge smile on her face, nodded and said, 'Yes… yes, that's what I'll do, I'll rescue the cat.'

16

ELEANOR
RESCUES THE CAT

Lucy watched, open-mouthed, as Eleanor, without hesitation, stepped boldly into the crowd and said, 'I'll get it down!'

Everyone stopped talking and turned their heads in her direction at the same time, amazed – nobody had even realised she was there. Then giggling started, followed by loud laughter, and then jeering.

'As if!' someone commented.

This was followed by, 'Look, it's Spider Girl, now she thinks she's Tarzan,' from someone else.

The laughter continued as Eleanor walked past them to the tree next to the one the cat was stuck in, and they laughed even louder as she jumped up and grabbed the first branch.

'Look, she's so stupid she's climbing the wrong tree,' another person said. But Eleanor was far from stupid and knew exactly what she was doing: she was going to rescue the cat!

Very quickly she had realised that the easiest route to it would be from the very thick branch near the top of the tree she was now climbing; if she could get there she would be able to reach across to the next tree where the cat was sitting, petrified.

Lucy was now back in the bubble, getting a much better view, and watched as Eleanor climbed higher and higher, reaching and pulling herself up from branch to branch. Grey squirrels scattered out of her way as she did so; this was their territory and they weren't used to seeing humans up this high, the occasional silly cat maybe, but not humans. Down below the laughter had stopped; all that could be heard were things like, 'Wow!' and, 'Isn't she amazing!' and, 'I wish I was as brave as that!'

By the time she got within reach of the cat, the crowd had grown considerably as people rushed to see what everyone was looking up at. Most expected it to be a rare bird that had flown in from another country, and one man who was a photographer had come to join them.

Now most cats in this situation, when they are really frightened and someone strange is trying to

grab hold of them, would panic, try to get away and possibly fall out of the tree – but this cat didn't, it kept perfectly still, Horla had made sure of that!

Lucy looked on, confident in Horla's ability, yet with a nagging doubt, remembering she'd knocked a referee out trying to score a goal in a football match once, so she didn't always get it right.

She watched as Eleanor reached out and carefully lifted the cat off the branch and put it in her shoulder bag. As she did so, a big cheer came from the crowd down below.

Then came the really difficult part: getting back down to the ground. Gently, she pushed the bag round on to her back and, carefully, made her way across to the other tree. In the distance she could hear the sound of a siren.

Oh no, that sounds like a fire engine. I hope it hasn't been called because I'm at the top of this tree, she thought, *better get a move on or I'll be in for a right telling off for doing something dangerous.*

The children looking up at her, their mouths open like chicks waiting to be fed, knew that they couldn't do what she was doing and instead gazed admiringly, each one wishing they were her friend. On reaching the other tree, Eleanor very skilfully started to descend, using exactly the same branches she had used on the way up.

'Oh please be careful, Eleanor,' Lucy found herself saying, as she watched with her hands together as if in prayer. Unfortunately, she said it a little too loudly causing Horla to lose concentration.

She turned to Lucy and scolded her saying, '*Shush,* I'm trying to concentrate.'

As she said this, the crowd gasped in horror… because Eleanor had lost her footing and was plummeting towards the ground!

'*Cracker-doo-doos!'* Horla said, re-focussing on the situation as Eleanor tried but failed to grab branches as she was falling. To the people looking on it seemed a hopeless situation until, seconds from certain death, she did grab a branch, then swung like an orang-utan to another, then another and another until she reached the bottom branch where two adults, so relieved she was still in one piece, reached to help her down. Although she didn't need their help, she took their hands anyway and jumped down to the ground. As she did so everyone in the crowd started clapping; it had been so expertly done that they actually thought she'd fallen deliberately to show off her acrobatic skills.

'Well *that* ought to impress her classmates,' Horla chuckled.

'*Phew*,' Lucy said, 'it certainly should.'

And they were right, because Emily rushed up to Eleanor and said, 'Thank you *so* much for rescuing my cat Tinker, you are so amazing.'

'Yes you are,' said Emily's friend, Jemima, adding, 'I couldn't have done *anything* as brave as that – you were just incredible!'

Then the rest of Emily's friends joined in congratulating Eleanor for having the courage to do what she did. At this point, a certain little dog hovering above was showing signs of being desperate for a pee.

'I think it would be a good idea to let him water a tree before we head off home, don't you,' Lucy said, nodding in Pip's direction.

'Good idea, we could all do with stretching our legs before we set off,' Horla replied, setting the bubble in motion towards the quiet area amongst some trees they had used minutes earlier. Pip was very happy to be back on the ground, but no sooner had he relieved himself than a fire engine arrived.

'Come on, let's take a closer look,' Horla said at the sight of the big red engine.

Emily, feeling really, really happy, dashed over with her cat in her arms to the firemen and said, 'It's OK, we don't need you now, because my cat's already been rescued,' and pointing to Eleanor, continued, 'she went to the very top of that tree and brought Tinker back down for me.'

Captain Chapman, the fireman in charge looked across at Eleanor. Knowing he should tell her off for doing something that was very dangerous indeed, he made his way over to have a word with her. However, before he reached her, he was interrupted by a group of adults all wanting to tell him what they had just witnessed.

'That was the bravest thing I have ever seen a child do,' said one.

'Extraordinary bravery for one so young, she obviously cares about animals,' said another.

Then the photographer showed him a video of the whole event saying, 'It was without doubt one of the most skilful pieces of climbing I have witnessed in my entire life!'

On hearing all this, Captain Chapman thanked the people for the information and continued across to Eleanor, who, on seeing his approach, felt sure she was about to get a ticking off.

'Can I have your name and address please?' he asked. In a timid voice, she told him – then waited like a naughty pupil outside the headmaster's office as he wrote down the details. To her great surprise, he then said out loud so everyone could hear, 'Well Eleanor, I've not only heard about your bravery, but seen it too, therefore I am going to recommend you for a Good Citizen's Award, one of the fire brigade's top bravery honours for civilians.'

'*Yesss!*' Lucy found herself saying, so thrilled for her friend. Eleanor's face went the colour of beetroot as people started clapping and rushed to shake her hand. Lucy laughed, saying, 'Just look at her face; I haven't seen it that colour since the time her skirt got stuck on a slide and everyone saw her knickers.'

Lucy, Horla and Pip then went closer and overheard Emily say, 'You're the new girl in our school aren't you?'

'Yes, I am,' replied Eleanor, stroking Tinker as she said it.

'Would you like to come to my house and play sometime? My parents would be really pleased to see you after I tell them how you rescued Tinker.'

'Yes, I'd really like that,' Eleanor answered, with a huge grin on her face.

Lucy was really pleased on hearing that and, standing on tip-toe a few metres away, tried to catch her friend's eye. Suddenly, Pip, recognising it was Eleanor in the midst of the crowd, gave a quick bark of excitement, then barged his way through to her, dragging Lucy with him.

'*Pip!*' Eleanor squealed in delight as he came into view, tail wagging furiously: a few minutes earlier she had been so miserable – now she couldn't be happier.

'This is my friend Lucy and her grandma's dog, Pip,' she announced proudly to her new friends, who, after brief, "Hellos", all crowded round to make a fuss of Pip (apart from Tinker that is, who, in Emily's arms, just hissed in his direction).

As their attention was drawn to Pip, Lucy said, 'I have to get back, Elle, so I'll leave you with your new friends.'

Eleanor beamed; she was glad Lucy was pleased for her, that's why she was her best friend. Then she said, 'But I still can't understand – how did you get here so quickly?'

'I can't tell you in front of all these people, and besides, you wouldn't believe me if I told you anyway.'

'No, you definitely wouldn't believe her,' a voice said with a giggle.

Eleanor's eyes widened: she looked round, puzzled, wondering who had said that, but everyone was fussing over Pip.

'Now I really must go,' Lucy said, trying not to laugh, 'but remember, don't say a word to anyone about me being here.'

'Okaaay… I really would like to know though!'

Lucy smiled, 'I suspect you'll coax it out of me one day,' she said, 'anyway, I'm going – let me know how you get on at school next week.'

'OK, I will.'

'Good – now you get talking to your friends, they'll want to know all about you.'

Eleanor smiled once again and gave Lucy a parting hug.

'Bye,' said Lucy.

'Bye,' said Eleanor.

'Bye,' said the voice.

Looking mystified, Eleanor said, 'Have you been practising ventriloquism?'

Lucy couldn't hold it any longer and burst out laughing. She pulled Pip away from the group, saying, 'Bye everyone, see you next time,' and walked off to a chorus of, 'Bye Lucy,' ringing in her ears.

'Well,' said Horla, as they headed back towards the quiet area amongst the trees, 'Eleanor's made some friends now, so I'd call that mission accomplished, wouldn't you?'

'Yes, I agree,' said a beaming Lucy, 'you did a good job.'

'And you did too… for a ventriloquist!'

'Ha ha, that was funny, but how am I going to explain me being here when a short while ago I was hundreds of miles away?'

'You won't have to.'

'Won't I?'

'No. Come on, pick up Pip… one, two, three jump!'

Seconds later, Horla had manoeuvred the bubble above Eleanor and her new friends.

'Now, Lucy, please be quiet for a moment while I concentrate,' she said, seriously.

'OK, Mum, will do,' Lucy replied, jokingly.

But Horla didn't see the funny side; she had immediately gone into concentration mode and was staring intently at Eleanor and her new friends, busy chatting away below. Nobody noticed that the group froze and stopped chatting, for it only lasted a few seconds, before they carried on as if nothing had happened.

'That ought to do it,' Horla then said with a smile of satisfaction, 'she won't even know you've been.'

'Great, now we'd better get back home, before Mum and Grandma get concerned about me.'

'Don't worry, they won't be concerned, once we get going I'll tell you what they've been up to.'

17

THE "DANCING IN WATER" INCIDENT

Once the bubble had started speeding towards Lucy's local park, Horla proceeded to tell Lucy of what was going on when she was doing her "Nearly Headless Nick" impersonation.

After she and her two companions had left for Liverpool, Mum and Grandma, who had forgotten the purpose of coming to the park, had sauntered along, completely oblivious of the time. They enjoyed the walk so much that every time there was a diversion in the paths, they always chose the path that would extend the length of the walk. And it was while walking along, and chatting, that something really pleasing caught their eye. Up ahead, a mother (who Grandma thought later as not the brightest person she'd ever met) was pushing a pram, while holding the reins of her toddler, walking alongside dressed in a pink all-in-one suit.

'Ah,' Grandma said, 'that reminds me of you a few years ago.'

Her daughter chuckled and replied, 'Yes, you're right, that could be me if the clock were wound back; if you remember, once Lucy started walking, she refused to get in the pram, until she wore herself out of course.'

'I remember all right. I also remember trying to get her into a suit like that little one's wearing, when she was about ten months old.'

'Oh that *was* funny.'

'Yes it was. I would put one leg in, then as I tried to put the other one in, Lucy would take the first one out; she thought it was a game and giggled her little head off.'

The two ladies were smiling at the thought of the younger Lucy's antics as they neared the mother and toddler. The mother, at that moment, was multi-tasking: with her left hand, she pushed the pram and held on to the reins of the toddler, with her right hand she used a mobile phone, operating it with a thumb that moved at incredible speed.

Suddenly the little girl sneezed, and green snot burst out of her nostrils and hung down like two stalactites in a cave. In an instant, her mother put her phone on the pram, whisked out a tissue and wiped the child's nose. She then pleaded with her to blow, but the child was having none of it, and instead moved her head from side to side and danced on the spot in a tantrum. Just then, with the mum's back turned, the pram, being on a slight slope and helped by a mysterious sudden gust of wind, started rolling towards the lake. Grandma, who despite being almost eighty and not having the best of eyesight, was the first to notice.

'Is that pram moving, or am I seeing things?' she asked.

'Oh my word, so it is,' Lucy's mum replied, then shouted: 'The pram – the pram!'

The mother, alerted, turned around just in time to see the pram slowly roll into the water and float out of her reach. She screamed, which frightened the toddler, causing her to burst into tears. Lucy's mum and grandma quickly arrived and tried to calm the distraught woman.

'My mobile, my mobile, it's in the pram,' she wailed.

'Don't worry, I'm sure we'll be able to get the pram out one way or the other, and it will soon dry out,' Lucy's mum said trying to calm her.

'Yes, but what about my mobile, it could be ruined, what about Twitter, how am I going to tweet without it!' she sobbed, dabbing her mascara with the same tissue she'd used to wipe up the snot.

Grandma, looking at the woman, whose eyes now resembled a panda's, whispered to her own daughter, 'We've got a right one here... she thinks she's a bird and wants to tweet to her friend Twitter.'

'No, Mum, it's not like that...' her daughter replied, about to educate her elderly mother on the workings of social media. Her voice trailed off as she realised the pram's hood was acting as a sail in the wind, which was pushing the pram further away from them.

Grandma saw this and casually remarked, 'That pram wouldn't be difficult to get to you know; I've seen the lake drained and although it's deep in the middle, it's quite shallow near the edge.'

'Right,' her daughter replied, 'I've got my old walking shoes on so I'm going to turn up my trouser legs and go in and get it.'

'That's my girl!' Grandma said proudly.

And Lucy's mum did exactly that: she turned up her trouser legs above her knees and walked in – not realising that the edging stones under the water were slimy, and very, very slippery!

Splash! she went, as her feet came from under her and she landed in the lake, bottom-first. Grandma was right: it wasn't deep at all, when you're standing up that is. Seeing her sitting there, water up to her waist, a university student on a bike quickly dismounted and, without hesitation, waded in to

help her, also not realising that the edging stones under the water were slimy, and very, very slippery!

Splash! he went, as *his* feet came from under *him* and *he* landed bottom-first... on Lucy's mum's lap.

While all this was going on, the toddler, who had by now stopped crying, watched mesmerised at the goings on; she couldn't wait to be a grown-up, it seemed so much fun. Her mother, meanwhile, was getting desperate because she hadn't been on Twitter for nearly five minutes.

Up in the bubble, Lucy, on hearing this, laughed out loud at the comical situation her mum had found herself in, which was exactly what Grandma did at the scene.

Trying to keep a straight face at the hilarious sight of her daughter and the student splashing around like two children in a bath, she couldn't contain herself any longer as the pair of them, holding on to each other, attempted to stand up. The student rose first, on all fours to begin with, then expanding to his full height, he held out his hands to Lucy's mum who gratefully took them. And that's when the fun really started.

Obviously thinking that Lucy's mum was heavier than she was, he pulled with all his might and she shot up like a jack-in-the-box and crashed into him. This caused them both to lose balance again and, in a desperate effort to stay upright on the slippery surface, they clung on to each other's arms, while their legs carried out the most unusual actions. Grandma was a big fan of *Strictly Come Dancing*; she was also a fan of *Dancing on Ice*; now she was rapidly becoming a fan of "Dancing in Water", and this was much funnier than the other two.

She burst out laughing as they steadied themselves, looking like a pair of wrestlers trying to throw each other in a ring. The pram, meanwhile, was mysteriously blown back, handle first, to the side of the lake where the young mother pulled it out, relieved that her mobile phone wasn't damaged. She immediately set about telling the world of her recent experience, while her daughter walked off, sat down next to Grandma, and clapped the two adults in the water providing the entertainment for her. She watched as the performers, still holding on to each other, side-stepped like a single giant crab back onto the path, dripping and laughing after their unexpected encounter.

'Come on, Louise, better get home and out of those wet clothes before you freeze to death,' Grandma said.

'You're right, Mum,' her daughter replied, before adding to the student, 'well, nice to have met you. If I ever decide to take up synchronised swimming, I'll know where to come for a partner.'

'You're on,' laughed the student, mounting his bike and giving a cheery wave as he pedalled off into the distance, dripping water as he went. Then without a single thought in their head about Lucy, her relatives set off for their respective homes, with her mum dripping water that left a trail any self-respecting slug would be proud of.

***

Lucy's mum arrived home first and, having changed out of the wet clothing, was brought back to reality on hearing the phone ring. It was Grandma who, having got back home and taken off her coat, had snapped out of her short-term amnesia. For the second time that day, the short conversation was repeated:

'Hi, Mum.'

'Hi, Louise, they've just left.'

'OK, you set off and I'll meet you at the park gates.'

'OK, see you there.'

A short time later, the three adventurers arrived back to find Mum and Grandma scratching their heads and wondering where on earth Lucy and Pip could be. Manoeuvring between some trees a little bit behind them, the bubble touched down and Lucy and Pip reappeared.

'Hi, Mum, hi, Grandma,' Lucy shouted as she set off to run to them. But Pip had other ideas; he was ready for another pee and almost pulled Lucy's arm off as he raced to the nearest tree and proceeded to cock his leg. Mum and Grandma walked quickly back to them and both asked the same question at the same time: 'Where have you been?' This was followed by, 'We've been looking all over for you,' from Grandma.

'Oh, here and there,' said Lucy, 'but why were you looking for me?'

'Oh, erm, we decided to have a walk ourselves and thought we might bump into you, that's all,' Mum lied.

Chill yer beans, yer can't kid me, Lucy thought, laughing inside at her mum's explanation.

The adults, though, were so relieved that they were safe and didn't ask any more awkward questions, instead they all headed home to Grandma's for tea and biscuits and a doggy treat for Pip.

18

THE "STRANGE COINCIDENCE" OF LUCY'S DOUBLE

On Monday after school, Lucy got in her mum's car to be told, in an astonished voice, 'Lucy, you are never going to believe what Eleanor's been up to!'

'What's that Mum?' she replied, innocently.

'I've just checked my Facebook account, and there's a photo of her on the front page of the *Liverpool Echo.*'

'*Really?*'

'Yes, and she's at the top of a massive tree!'

'Flippin' heck, what's she doing up there?'

'She rescued a cat, would you believe?'

'Wow, that was a brave thing to do.'

'There's nothing brave about that – she could have got herself killed!'

'Do you think so?'

'*I know so*; it's silly to go so high in the air without something firm beneath your feet.'

'Oh I'd never go high in the air without something firm beneath *my* feet!'

'*I'm glad to hear it!*'

Lucy thought for a moment, and then said, 'I need to use your iPad to do my maths homework; can I Skype Eleanor after that and find out all about it?'

'Yes, of course you can, as long as you do your homework first.'

'No worries, Mum, I will.'

Arriving home, Lucy went straight to the bathroom and, within seconds, Horla appeared in the mirror.

'Hi, Horla,' she said, 'guess what, my mum knows about Eleanor rescuing the cat.'

'Cor, news travels fast on planet Earth,' Horla joked in reply.

'It certainly does. Mum says that after I've done my homework I can use her iPad to speak to Eleanor and ask her all about it.'

'Eye pad? You're going to speak to Eleanor using an eye pad!'

Lucy chuckled, realising the confusion in Horla's voice.

'Sorry, I'd forgotten, I've not shown you an iPad before, have I?' she said.

'You don't have to; I know what an eye pad looks like, I've even worn one, but I've never spoken through one though!'

'Ha ha, you'll understand what I'm talking about when I speak to Eleanor later – it should be a very interesting conversation!'

'Yes, very interesting; don't tell me she'll be speaking to *you* using an eye pad too?'

'Yes, actually, she will.'

'Oh, this I've got to see!'

Lucy laughed, saying, 'OK, see you later, about seven o'clock.'

'Can't wait,' Horla replied, shaking her head; 'speaking through eye pads, *how weird!*'

Lucy smiled as Horla disappeared from the mirror.

Just as well I didn't say I was using a "tablet" to speak to her, she thought.

***

At exactly seven o'clock, Horla appeared and Lucy told her to come into her room, rather than be spotted looking out of the mirror by Eleanor. After a quick explanation of how Skype works, and an uttering of, *'We are sooo behind planet Earth,'* by Horla, Lucy contacted Eleanor.

'Hello, my cat rescuer friend,' she said, smiling, as Eleanor came on the screen.

'Oh, Lucy, you've heard!'

'Yes I have, *you little monkey* – my mum picked it up on Facebook; so tell me all about it.'

'Well, I've had the most fantastic weekend.'

'It sounds like it, so c'mon spill the beans on the cat rescue.'

'Well, on Saturday I was in the park when I noticed some girls from my school. They were looking up at a cat at the top of a very tall tree, which belonged to a girl called Emily who is in my year at school.'

'The tree belonged to Emily?'

'Ha ha, very funny, it's good to know you haven't lost your sense of humour. Anyway, as I was saying, she had called the fire brigade but they were too busy to come and she was really worried her cat might fall out of the tree.'

'So you rescued it?'

'Yes, I climbed up the tree and brought it down.'

'Wow! I'll bet you're her hero now.'

'Well, sort of; she and I are friends now, and her friends have become my friends too.'

'That's fantastic.'

'Yes it is, and Emily invited me to her house on Sunday and we played loads of games.'

'Oh even better! And what about the photograph Mum told me about?'

'That was in the *Liverpool Echo*; the headline said, "Is this the bravest girl in Liverpool?"'

'Really?'

'Yes, my parents almost had a fit when they read it. They said it was a silly thing to have done, and never to do it again. The funny thing is, I don't think I *could* do it again because I don't feel that brave any more. I just don't know what came over me on Saturday; I felt as though I could do anything and I've no idea why. Still, climbing the tree got me new friends, so it was worth it.'

'It certainly was!'

'Oh, and you were right about Betty.'

'What do you mean?'

'They saw her when Mum picked me up and they think she's fantastic too.'

'Who is, your mum or Betty?'

'Stop it!'

'I'm only asking...'

'But do you know one other very strange thing about Saturday?'

'No, what was that?'

'Well, and I know you're going to find this weird, but since Saturday, several people who were in the park when I rescued Emily's cat have been asking us – that's me, Emily, Jemima and the rest of my new friends – who the girl with the dog was.'

'I don't get you.'

'Well, they say, and trust me, *this did not happen* – that I spoke to a girl with a Jack Russell dog, and we all stroked the dog – but we know we didn't, yet they keep saying we did.'

'It's probably a case of mistaken identity.'

'Yes, that's what I said, but here's the really weird bit, they say that when we said goodbye to them*, we called them Lucy and Pip!*'

'Wow, what a coincidence!'

'But that's not all.'

'No?'

'No! When we asked them to describe the girl and the dog, they could have been describing you and Pip, *in fact,* the dog even had one brown ear and one white ear just like Pip!'

'Ha ha, so Pip and I have doubles in Liverpool – that's amazing!'

'Yes, it sounds like it – but we *didn't* see them, no matter what people have said.'

'I believe you.'

'Anyway, I don't suppose you've done anything as interesting.'

'No I haven't, although I am allowed to take Pip out on my own now.'

'Oh that's good; where have you taken him to?'

'Well, I've only taken him to a couple of parks so far.'

'Oh he'll like that, just you and him alone enjoying yourselves, like the two great pals that you are. You know, it seems like *ages* since *we* last saw one another.'

'Hmm, yes it does.'

'Why are you smiling?'

'Oh, uh, nothing... I was just imagining you rescuing Tinker, that's all... I mean, well, it must have been great to watch.'

'I suppose so... but hang on, how did you know his name was Tinker?'

'Oh, erm... because you told me it was, that's how.'

'Did I?'

'Yes, of course you did, just now, I mean, how else would I know?'

'Sorry, you're right, I must have done, silly me. I'm not thinking straight; it's been such a strange last couple of days.'

'Ha ha, I bet it has, and I'll bet it's been better at school today than it was last week.'

'Oh, yes, *today was brilliant!*'

'Right then, I'm going to lie back on the bed and you can tell me all about it!'

And that's exactly what Lucy did... and so did Horla. Side by side they listened as Eleanor talked on about her new school, giving a far different version than that she'd given on Saturday: it was clear that she was now a very happy pupil, and it was all because she now had friends.

Eventually the girls said their goodbyes and promised to keep in touch with each other, Eleanor ending by saying, 'I'll really work on my mum and dad to get you that invitation to Liverpool.'

'Oh that'll be good – and go to the safari park?'

'Yes definitely.'

'But then again, that might not be such a good idea.'

'How do you mean?'

'Well, you being half monkey, they may not let you back out!'

'Ha ha, very funny indeed! Now I really must go, speak soon, bye.'

'OK, bye, Elle, speak soon.'

***

Later, Lucy sat at her dressing table mirror discussing with Horla the conversation she'd had earlier with Eleanor.

'So, it's been ages since you last saw one another hmm?' Horla said.

Lucy laughed, 'Yes, and it's ages since I've done anything interesting!'

'Oh it was so funny hearing her say that.'

'Yes, that's what I thought; it was a struggle not to laugh when I heard it.'

'It was for me too, although it wouldn't have been so funny if she'd known about me.'

'Yes, that's what I was thinking, so I'm not going to tell her about you.'

'You're *never* going to tell her about me?'

'No… well not for the time being anyway, because… well, if I'm honest, I rather like having you to myself.'

'Oooh, you're making me feel special now.'

'You are.'

'Stop it – you'll have *me* going the colour of beetroot next!'

'Ha ha, I can't imagine that *ever* happening.'

'No, maybe not, but do you know, Lucy, I *really* enjoyed that adventure on Saturday.'

'So did I. Who'd have thought Pip and I could go to Liverpool and back without my mum and grandma realising.'

'I thought you'd like that, was it the best bit of the day for you?'

'Well, although so many unusual things happened this week, like Mr. Baker's hat doing a loop-the-loop and flying out of the shop; the pasty turning around and hitting Tayler Taylor in the face, and the talking sweets jumping out of Bob the Rob's pockets, I did think travelling in the bubble was best – it was like the best dream I've ever had, *except that it was real!*'

'Well maybe if you borrow Pip this Saturday, we could meet up again.'

'And go up in the bubble?'

'Yes, if there's a need to.'

'And play more tricks on people?'

'Yes of course we will, especially the *bad people,*' Horla emphasised, pulling a fiendish face, 'and besides, I need to go bottom-pinching, tangerine juggling and trolley filling which we'd planned, but never did, remember.'

Lucy laughed and said, 'Oh, I'd forgotten about that, and I need to use my magic bike and skates.'

'That's settled then; I'll go now and leave you to get working on Grandma.'

'OK, but before you go, let's do a high five!'

Lucy then watched with a smile on her face as Horla's raised hand came towards her... and vanished!

'High five!' Horla then said, looking on as Lucy tried to hit the invisible hand in her room. She missed on the first and second attempt, but succeeded on the third with a loud *SLAP!*

Horla's hand then reappeared on the end of her arm as she pulled it back into Ivarnio and waved it, saying, 'Bye everyone, see you tomorrow.'

Lucy looked round and, to her amazement, not only were Fred and Ollie waving goodbye, but so too was every cuddly toy that had a hand or a paw or a tail or a wing to wave. Lucy turned back, a smile on her face, to see Horla, her friend from another world, disappear – leaving her staring at her own reflection once more!

19

THE MYSTERY OF THE CAMERA AND THE BOY

The following day, Lucy and her mum arrived home from school to find a policeman standing at their front door.

'Oh, it's Carl,' Lucy's mum said on recognising him, 'you know, he picks Dad up sometimes to play five-a-side football on Wednesday nights.'

'Oh yes, he looks different in a policeman's uniform,' Lucy replied.

'Hi, Louise, hi, Lucy,' Carl said, greeting them with a big smile on his face.

Lucy and her mum greeted him back, then Carl explained how, six months earlier, Lucy's dad, Dave, had handed him a camera he had found.

'I took it to the station but as nobody has claimed it in all that time, the finder, in this case, your dad, Lucy, is entitled to keep it,' he said, adding, 'I'm working afternoon shifts and won't be playing football for a while so I thought I'd hand it back while I'm passing.'

Louise, very relieved that he hadn't brought bad news, took it from him and thanked him for calling with it.

As he made his way down the path, the memory of the day her dad brought the camera home came into Lucy's thoughts; she remembered seeing the photographs on it and hoping it would be claimed as the family, whoever they were, seemed quite poor and possibly couldn't afford a replacement. As the photos of six months ago were going through her head, she suddenly had another thought and a plan began forming in her mind. She was realising that, after the adventure of the previous Saturday, there *was* a way to find the people on the photographs after all, and, with Horla's help, she was going to do just that.

Once in the house, Lucy made her way to the bathroom where, within seconds of her turning on the tap, Horla's smiling face appeared in the mirror.

'Hi, Lucy, have you had a good day at school? Not been troubled by those horrible Taylor triplets I hope,' she said.

'Yes, Horla, it was quite a good day, and no, that lot never troubled me at all, in fact they were very quiet and left everyone alone, how long that will last though, I'm not sure, but I did have a bit of a scare when I got home.'

'Why, what happened?'

'Well Mum and I arrived to find a policeman standing on our doorstep.'

'Did you?'

'Yes, we thought something awful had happened to Dad or Grandma, but it turned out to be nothing of the sort.'

'What had he called for then?'

'Well, to our surprise, he'd come to drop off something that *now* belongs to Dad.'

'Ooh, don't tell me, don't tell me… you know I like guessing games… that *now* belongs to your dad, hmm let me see… I know, I know, he's bought a second-hand police car?'

'Ha ha, no he hasn't.'

'Police motorbike then?'

'No silly.'

'Police helicopter?'

'Now that's even sillier.'

'Got it – it's a police horse isn't it?'

'Oh now you *are* being ridiculous.'

'I know, that's my middle name!'

Lucy laughed and said, 'Anyway, *"Ridiculous"*, it's none of those, but it is something I think you'll be really interested in, but it will have to wait until I've had my refreshments cos' I'm starving.'

'Okaaay… I think I can wait that long – you go and stuff your face and I'll see you in a bit.'

'OK, say about half an hour?'

'OK, half an hour, then you'll put me in the picture?'

'Ha ha, yes, then I'll put you in the picture!'

***

Half an hour later, and after a snack and a talk with her mum about how school had been that day, Lucy sat at her dressing table mirror explaining why the policeman had called earlier.

'It turned out that the policeman was my dad's friend, Carl, and he was returning a camera with photographs on that Dad had found and passed to him to hand in to the police station. That was six months ago and as it hadn't been claimed in all that time, Dad is allowed to keep it.'

To her delight, Horla reacted exactly as she hoped she would. With an excited look on her face she exclaimed, 'That's a shame it hasn't been claimed, but if you print off a photograph, we could find the person on it like we found Eleanor and *they* would know who owned it!'

'That's exactly what I thought you would say, Horla, so when Dad comes home from work I'll ask him to print off some of a boy who was on it; he looked ever so sad and I'd love to know why.'

'What, you mean he wasn't smiling when his picture was taken?'

'No, strange that, isn't it?'

'Yes, very strange, everyone smiles when they have their picture taken.'

'Well this boy didn't.'

'Hmm, I wonder why not?'

'I don't know, it's a bit of a mystery that we need to get to the bottom of,' Lucy replied seriously, sounding more like a policeman than Carl did.

'We could go looking for him on Saturday if you get permission to take Pip out again.'

'Oh sorry, I forgot to say that Grandma's given me permission; I spoke to her before I left for school this morning. She must trust me now because she immediately said yes.'

'Fantastic, all we need now is the photograph and we'll be off on another adventure.'

Lucy's face lit up on hearing the word "adventure" and she replied, 'OK, I'll speak to Dad as soon as he comes home; I've already worked out what I'm going to say so I'll come back later and let you know how I get on.'

***

When her dad arrived home from work, Lucy rushed to greet him and, after giving him a hug, passed him his slippers as he took off his shoes. She often did this, but this time she was a little more eager than usual as she had an important question to ask him.

'Dad, you know that camera you found that Carl took to the police station?' she said.

'Yes,' he replied with a puzzled look on his face, just about remembering.

'Well, it's been returned; can I have it please?'

'Whoa, hang on, what do you mean returned?'

'Carl brought it back today because nobody had claimed it and said because you found it, you can keep it.' Then she said again, 'So please can I have it, Dad? You and Mum both have cameras so you don't need *another* one.'

Her dad thought for a moment then said, 'I don't see why not, but if I remember correctly, there were photos on it weren't there?'

'Yes, Dad, that's right, there *are* photos on it, I had another look at them before you came home.'

'In that case I'll delete them and the camera will be as good as new.'

'*No, Dad, don't do that!*' Lucy exclaimed rather forcefully. 'I might be able to find the owner!'

'Oh and how do you propose to do that then, smarty pants?'

'Well I was thinking, if you were to print me some of the photos of a little boy on it, I could take them to school and someone there might recognise him.'

'What a good idea; you really *are* a smarty pants. OK, I'll print you some after tea, how's that?'

'That's great, Dad, thank you,' Lucy replied gratefully.

Later on, as promised, her dad printed the photographs and handed both the camera and prints to her saying, 'Here you are, Inspector, I hope your investigation is successful and you get your man.'

'Thanks, Dad, I'll try my very best,' she said with a huge grin on her face. The first part of the plan was complete.

20

THE SEARCH FOR
THE BOY STARTS

By the time Saturday came around, it had been arranged for Lucy to pick Pip up after lunch and take him for a walk in the park as she had done the previous week. In readiness, she packed her rucksack, putting in the camera and photographs plus some sweets and an umbrella in case it rained.

'I never know who I might meet in the park, Mum, so it's just possible I might meet the boy in the photograph, isn't it?' she had said as her mum noticed her packing it.

Her mum just chuckled to herself, thinking, *She's really taking this seriously*, feeling ever so proud of her caring daughter.

'Make sure you wear your watch so you can keep track of time, oh, and here, take my mobile phone with you so you can tell me the good news when you find him, but be careful though not to lose it.'

This really pleased Lucy; her mum had always told her she wasn't old enough to have a mobile and now here she was letting her borrow hers, but of course the real reason for that was so she could ring her daughter if she was worried about her, as neither she nor Grandma were going to follow her as they had the previous week. Lucy realised but didn't say anything; she just looked forward to bragging about it at school on Monday morning.

When lunch was over and the time had come, Lucy went upstairs to her room. She closed the door, went to the dressing table and moved everything off it. She finished doing this just as Horla appeared in the mirror.

'Ready?' she said.

'Yes,' Lucy replied.

'Right, stand by then, here I come.'

Schlluuuuuuppppp, then went the low, creepy sucking sound and within seconds Horla was in the bedroom squeezing Lucy's hand.

'OK, let's get these things back on the dressing table,' she said, knowing Lucy would once again enjoy what was coming next.

'Hairbrush on the left, remember,' Lucy reminded her.

'OK, *"Lefty"*, here we go.'

Lucy, delighted, watched again as the pieces rose off the bed into the air and flew over to the dressing table, landing ever so gently in all the right places. She smiled as she heard her mum downstairs, imagining the look on her face if she ever walked in while all this was happening.

'Right, now that's sorted, let's get this rucksack on my back and get going,' she said. But Horla had already gone; she'd opened the door and was sliding down the banister, completely forgetting herself, shouting, *'Wheee!'*

'Lucy, if you need to go for a wee, just go; there's no need to tell the whole world about it!' was shouted from the living room.

'Sorry, Mum, I'm so excited about taking Pip out that I slid down the banister,' Lucy answered.

'You slid down the banister! So that's what you do when you get excited; you'd better not get excited too often or you'll wear out the paint!'

'Ha ha, very funny, Mum,' Lucy replied, while opening the door so Horla could slip out. 'Anyway,' she continued, 'I'm off now to pick up Grandma's *little rascal.'*

'OK,' Mum said, coming out of the sitting room, 'be careful crossing the roads to the park and *don't stay out too long,'* she emphasised.

'Message understood, Mum,' Lucy said, stepping out of the door. 'See you later.'

'See you later,' her mum replied, shaking her head and smiling warmly.

★★★

A short while later, Grandma watched from her window as Lucy and Pip went on their way to the park. 'She's definitely been teaching him tricks,' she said, smiling to herself as she saw Pip, once again, standing on his back legs, leaning against nothing but fresh air, wagging his tail furiously. Then, as if glimpsing into the future, she added, 'She'll be entering him in a talent show next!'

★★★

Within minutes of leaving Grandma's house, Horla saw something she had never seen before. Walking in front of them was a boy eating a bag of crisps. When he finished them, he threw the empty bag on the ground, even though there was a litter bin nearby, and just walked on. She was flabbergasted.

'Did you see that,' she said, 'why didn't he put it in the bin or take it home with him?'

'Unfortunately, some people are so lazy, that's what they do,' replied Lucy, with a sigh.

'Well now, what can I do to make him think twice about doing it again,' Horla pondered.

Lucy didn't answer, but instead smiled, wondering what was going to happen next.

'Got it,' Horla said triumphantly.

Seconds later, the crisp bag lifted off the ground and flew into the boy's left coat pocket. A look of surprise came over his face and he quickly pulled it out and threw it down again. Immediately, the bag rose up, and this time shot into his right coat pocket. The boy by now didn't know what was going on and threw the bag on the ground for the third time. This time it shot up in front of his face with the open end towards him and formed the shape of a mouth. It then started moving like a mouth and said, *'Put me in the bin, put me in the bin!'*

The boy tried to move away in different directions but still it stayed in front of his face saying louder and louder, *'Put me in the bin, put me in the bin!'*

By now a crowd was gathering. They didn't know how the boy was doing it but they thought he was a really good magician. They joined in and, before he knew it, there were about forty people shouting along with the bag, *'Put me in the bin put me in the bin!'*

The boy was so embarrassed that his face turned bright red. All he wanted to do was get as far away from there as soon as possible and the best thing to do was to put the bag in the bin. He reached into the air and got hold of the bag between his finger and thumb, as if it were some hairy scary spider, and dropped it in the bin. As he did so, all the people clapped him, as they thought he'd just put on a wonderful performance. The boy, though, was totally confused, and turned and ran home as fast as his legs would carry him.

'Well, I don't think he'll be dropping litter again anytime soon!' Horla said. Both girls burst out laughing and continued on their way.

***

Within no time at all they had reached the park and were heading down the main path to the café when they saw something that really upset them. In the park there are a lot of squirrels and sometimes, after a stormy night, they sit on the grass eating nuts that have been blown down from the trees. To the girls' horror, running around under a group of trees was a dog, a really vicious, ugly-looking dog, with an owner who could have been its twin, screaming at it to chase and catch a squirrel. As one squirrel managed to escape up a tree, the dog would go on to chase another, and the girls were convinced that sooner or later it would kill one of the cute little creatures.

'Hmm, I reckon our furry friends could do with a bit of help, don't you?' Horla remarked surveying the scene.

'They certainly could,' Lucy said in agreement.

'Right then, let's get them organised!'

Lucy didn't know what was going to happen next, but she knew it was going to be exciting, and what did happen took even her by surprise. First she noticed that there was movement in the tops of the trees near the ugly man with the ugly dog. Then she realised why: the trees were coming alive with squirrels!

From all over the park they came, jumping from branch to branch until every squirrel in the park reached the trees where their friends were being chased. They surrounded the man and the dog, and then the most unexpected thing happened: they started throwing acorns at them, then horse chestnuts, then bits of loose branches, in fact, anything that could be thrown was thrown. It was amazing how accurate they were and how hard they could throw things.

Down below the man was yelling, *'Ow, ow, ow!'* (plus other rude words adults sometimes use) and the dog was yelping in pain as they were being hit by the objects being hurled at them. People walking by stopped and looked on in amazement. They started cheering the squirrels, then laughed out loud as the man, who had decided to run as fast as he could from under the trees, slipped on the nuts and fell flat on his face. He got up and ran to the path at the side of the lake with his dog scampering after him, thinking his troubles were over – but he was wrong!

Up above, high in the sky, a flock of Canadian geese were flying in a V formation, making their way to a nearby wetland centre. Noticing them, Horla said, 'Ooh, I'm sure those geese would like to give the squirrels a hand, Lucy'.

Lucy gazed upwards in time to see the geese suddenly change to single file and alter their direction so that they were now flying towards the park. Down and down they came as if they were going to land in the lake. Then, at the last moment, they changed direction again and flew straight towards the ugly man and his ugly dog. Then Lucy could not believe her ears when she heard the front goose say, 'Right squadron, target identified; lock on and bombs away!'

'Roger that,' was the reply from the rest of the geese. No sooner was this said than she heard, *SPLAT, SPLAT, SPLAT, SPLAT, SPLAT,* as the

geese flew over the man's head, each one doing a poo on him. *SPLAT, SPLAT, SPLAT, SPLAT, SPLAT, SPLAT, SPLAT, SPLAT, SPLAT, SPLAT,* it went, on and on and on and on.

The man started running to get away and suddenly remembered he had a hood. He quickly pulled it up without realising that it was by now full of poo. It squashed onto his head, slithered down his neck, went under his shirt, continued down his back and into his underpants. Eventually, by the time the geese had flown back off into the sky, he looked like a snowman – not a white snowman; a green, slimy, horrible snowman, and he was smelly – very, very smelly!

Once he knew the geese had gone, he stopped running and stood still, exhausted, looking down at himself and thinking of what to do next. People who had seen what happened walked past holding their noses and saying, 'Oh what a pong, you ought to take a shower occasionally,' then laughing out loud as they went on their way.

'He deserves being made fun of,' another said, 'nasty piece of work that he is.'

Lucy and Horla watched as the man, realising he couldn't possibly walk home looking as he did, turned towards the lake and started to walk in. The ducks, moorhens and coots made way as he carried on until the water came up to his knees, then his waist, then his shoulders and eventually he took a deep breath and disappeared out of sight. He'd obviously thought that the best way to get rid of the poo was to rinse it off under the water. Then Horla noticed some little heads bobbing in the water and said, 'Am I seeing things, or are they terrapins?'

'They are,' said Lucy, 'Grandma says they are descendants of two dumped there years ago. Apparently they're quite nasty and eat the birds' eggs; they've even been known to eat the chicks.'

'Hmm, so they're nasty, he's nasty; I wonder who would win in a fight?'

Lucy chuckled and said, 'I don't know, but I've a feeling I'm about to find out.'

Seconds later the man's head popped up and he gave a loud scream.

'Ow, ow, ow, ow, ow, ow!' (and the other rude words) were heard, as six terrapins sunk their jaws

into his bottom. He tried to rush out of the water, but he wasn't fast enough, and they continued to nip his legs, then his ankles before finally, dripping wet and with a squelching noise coming from his shoes, he made it to the path.

'I think the squirrels and terrapins won that one, don't you?' giggled Horla as they watched the man skulk off home.

'Definitely, I can't see him wanting to mess with *them* again,' Lucy replied.

'Ha ha, no, I can't either, especially when there are geese flying overhead.'

Lucy laughed, but not too loudly as there were people approaching. 'Anyway,' she said quietly, 'we'd better get a move on now or we'll run out of time.'

Both girls then strode on quickly, giving Pip the occasional tug as he stopped to investigate the doggy smells, and soon they were at the back of the café.

'Right, you know what to do, Lucy,' Horla then said.

'Yes,' an excited Lucy replied, picking up Pip.

Then, as had happened the previous week, when they were sure nobody was looking, Horla said, 'OK – one, two, three, jump,' and Lucy, holding Pip, jumped up into the air and disappeared. This time Lucy knew what to expect. There they were with Horla, who had reappeared, rising higher and higher into the air, inside the bluey-grey bubble that nobody below could see. When it got above the trees, it stopped.

'OK, let me have that photo now, Lucy please, and we'll see where it takes us,' Horla said.

Lucy then reached into her rucksack and pulled out the picture of the boy. On handing it to Horla, the bubble started to move forwards, slowly at first then a little faster; then faster still, until it was speeding along, with the girls not knowing where they were going, only that they were heading to where the sad little boy in the photo lived.

21

THE SORRY TALE OF ALEX AND SPEEDY

Before very long the girls found themselves approaching the next town. Lucy recognised it as a place she first visited as a very little girl when she went to see Peppa Pig in pantomime, and she had visited it a few times since with her family on shopping trips.

The bubble started to slow down as it approached a rather run-down housing estate of very old derelict houses. Steadily, it made its way to one particular house, which stood out because others surrounding it had been demolished. It looked a sorry sight, standing there all alone. The girls suddenly realised that this was possibly the only one on the estate that was occupied as it had curtains on the windows, something that none of the others, as far as they could see, had. The bubble stopped outside the house and lowered down to the ground.

Checking nobody was about, Lucy and Pip suddenly reappeared. Pip, who was by now getting used to Horla disappearing, had a sniff to check she was still there, then toddled off to the nearest lamppost to have a pee. After giving him a moment, Lucy shortened his lead and pulled him closer, then walked up the steps to the front door and rang the bell.

Within seconds, the face of the very boy they were searching for appeared in the window. At the same time, they heard footsteps coming down the hall towards the door. With a loud creaking sound, the door was opened and a lady with a smiling face looked down on them.

'Hello,' she said cheerfully, and immediately bent over and stroked Pip affectionately; it was obvious she liked dogs. Pip gave a friendly bark and a wag of his tail, loving the attention as he always did.

As soon as he heard the bark, the boy came running along the hall and squeezed past the lady, saying, 'Excuse me, Mum,' and proceeded to make an even bigger fuss of Pip. His mum smiled at this scene; her son was never happier than when he was with dogs. Then she turned her attention to Lucy, wondering who this young girl was, and why she had called.

'Are you a friend of Alex's?' she said with a puzzled look on her face. 'I've not seen you at his school.'

'No, I'm not,' said Lucy, pulling the camera out of her rucksack. 'It's just that my dad found this camera and…'

'Oh my word, I never thought I'd ever see *that* again,' the lady said, immediately recognising it, 'I thought it was lost forever.'

Lucy beamed, so pleased the camera had been reunited with its owner. The lady, whose name was Mrs. Rusk, said she had lost it late the previous year while out searching for Alex's dog, Speedy, who had gone missing weeks earlier. The dog had never been found and her son hadn't been the same since, which, thought Lucy, was probably the reason for the sad face on the photograph.

She explained, 'Speedy was a greyhound that we found wandering the streets one day. He was desperately thin and we suspected he had previously been used for greyhound racing, and thought perhaps, because he wasn't now fast enough, had been thrown out by his owner. We even suspected he had been mistreated because he was very timid and wary when we tried to approach him. Eventually, and after a lot of coaxing, we managed to feed him some titbits and a drink of water, which he gulped down before running off, much to Alex's disappointment.'

'Yes, I was *really* disappointed,' the boy chipped in.

'Anyway, the following day, much to our delight, I opened the curtains to see the dog sitting outside on our steps. I remember being so pleased and shouting, "Alex, wake up, the dog's come back!"

'We rushed downstairs to open the door but this time we decided to be a little more cautious so as not to frighten him off. I opened the door and said a friendly "Hello" to him, but instead of going outside, we went into the kitchen to get him some food, purposely leaving the front door wide open as we did so. When we got back, the dog, although still wary and looking a little frightened, had stepped into the hall.'

'Yes, and his head was bowed low and his tail was between his legs, wasn't it, Mum?'

'It was, Alex, yes,' Mrs. Rusk replied wistfully. She then continued explaining how he slowly inched forward with big sad eyes looking upwards at them. The greyhound was so timid that they presumed it must have been a long time since he was shown any affection. It melted Alex's heart and he pleaded with his mum to let the greyhound stay with them.

"He may not want to stay," she had told him, but he did.

From that day on, Speedy never strayed from Alex's side, apart from when he went to school, and even then Speedy went to the school gates with Mrs. Rusk. He was the last thing Alex saw when he went into school and the first thing he saw when he came out: he really loved Speedy. They'd had such wonderful times playing in the park; no other dog could run as fast as he could and he always came back to Alex when he threw the ball. Always, that is, until one fateful day when he didn't!

'So he's disappeared you mean, and you haven't seen him since?' Lucy asked.

'Yes, that's right, he just disappeared, didn't he, Mum?' Alex quickly replied.

'Yes. It was one nice light evening and Alex had had his tea and done his homework so we set off with Speedy for his last walk of the day. We took a ball as we always did, and a plastic thrower so that the ball would go really far.'

'Oh they are really good those, aren't they? I'm going to buy Pip one out of my pocket money,' Lucy interrupted.

'Well, yes and no,' Mrs. Rusk continued. 'On this particular day the wind was behind the ball when Alex threw it, so it went very fast, and further than he had ever thrown it before.'

'It was my best throw ever, Mum.'

'Yes, it was, and Speedy set off to catch it but, unfortunately, there was another dog ahead and as the ball whizzed past it, the other dog also set off after the ball.'

'Blinkin' nuisance it was,' Alex added.

'You can say that again. Anyway, we saw Speedy catch up and then both dogs disappeared around a corner into a car park, and we haven't seen Speedy since. By the time we got to the car park he'd vanished.'

Lucy felt so sorry for Alex, who looked to the floor as the sad time was recalled, desperately holding back tears.

'Someone said they had seen two dogs get into a van,' Mrs. Rusk continued, 'but they couldn't be sure one of them was Speedy, as lots of people own two dogs and walk them in the park.'

'Yeah, some people have two dogs and I haven't even got one now,' Alex blurted out, unable to contain his emotions any longer.

'Well, we did try, didn't we, Alex? I mean, we carried on looking that night, shouting his name until eventually it got too dark to see and we had to give up, don't you remember?'

Alex, head still down, nodded in agreement.

'And while you were at school the following day, I continued the search, looking in the park and some of the surrounding roads, and in the evening we both went out to look; we were determined not to give up until we found him.'

'But we didn't, did we Mum?'

'No we didn't, and now the council are re-housing all the families on this estate, offering everyone brand new homes miles away. One by one our neighbours have moved out, but we've kept putting it off, hoping that Speedy would come home before we have to leave. Now we are the only ones left, and the council have insisted we move out by the end of the month. We've no alternative now, we have to go, whether Speedy has returned or not; it's very sad.'

'I don't want to go, Mum, not till he comes back,' Alex chipped in.

'I know you don't, Alex, which is why, Lucy, as a last resort, and even though I couldn't afford it, I paid to have some posters printed, which I've attached to trees around the park. They show a picture of Speedy and the phone number to ring if anyone knows where he is, but so far nobody has rung.'

As Mrs. Rusk finished saying this, Lucy felt a gentle tug at her sleeve, and realised that Horla was probably thinking exactly what she herself was thinking.

'Mrs. Rusk, have you got a spare poster we could have, I mean I could have?' she asked. 'Maybe I might have a bit of luck in finding him.'

Without hesitation, Alex immediately dashed down the hall and up the stairs to his bedroom, returning within seconds clutching a copy of the poster, his hopes that his beloved Speedy would be found, rising again.

Lucy then declined an invitation to go inside for a warm drink, as she realised time was moving on and there was more to do now before she made her way home. Pip, however, enjoyed a bowl of water and some dog biscuits, and being him, was looking up expectantly for more as he always did. Grandma was right: she'd always said he'd be the size of an elephant if he was allowed to eat whatever he wanted.

22

THE LIMESTONE PAVEMENT AND THE RUNNER

Lucy waved goodbye to Alex and his mum as she, Pip and Horla walked off down the road. They turned behind a derelict house and, after checking no one was about, Horla picked up Pip in preparation to jump up into the bubble.

Just then the phone rang. Lucy immediately reached into her rucksack and, realising it was her mum, excitedly told her about finding the owner of the camera. She also told her about Alex and how his dog had gone missing and how she was now going to try to find it, hardly pausing for breath as she spoke. Her mum congratulated her, but fortunately did not ask where the owner lived, which was just as well because she would have had a fit had she realised how far away her daughter was at that moment.

'Right, well don't search for too long, it'll be teatime shortly and Dad will be home with, "you-know-what".'

Lucy's taste buds sprung into life at the mention of "you-know-what", as her dad always brought home her favourite chocolate bar as a treat when he worked overtime at the weekends.

'OK, Mum, I won't be too long,' she replied.

As soon as the phone was back in the rucksack, Horla said, 'Come on, let's get a move on; on the count of three: one, two, three, jump!'

As Horla said this, a man taking a short cut on his way home from the pub turned round and headed back to the shopping centre where he knew there was an opticians; he had just seen a dog sitting in mid-air, and a little girl talking on a mobile phone, and now he could see neither – he definitely needed new glasses, he thought, either that or he would have to stop drinking beer... he hoped he needed new glasses!

With Horla holding the photograph of Speedy, the bubble rose slowly up above the houses. Once it got a lot higher than even the tallest chimney pot it started moving, slowly at first, then accelerating out

of town in the direction of the surrounding hills. The girls were expecting it to go on over into the next town but it didn't. As it got to the top of one of the hills, it started slowing down and came to a stop above an area of hard rock known as the Limestone Pavement.

'I've seen rock like this before, now where was it?' Lucy said, 'Ah yes, it was in a film called, *Harry Potter and the Deathly Hallows*, I watched it with Dad and he said the rock was 350 million years old.'

'Wow, that's old.'

'Yes, that's what I thought when he said it.'

'I'm surprised it's stopped here though, I mean, there's no dog to be seen.'

'Yes, you're right, and we're well away from any paths that a person or dog would take.'

'Hmm, there's no point getting out here, but… well I just can't understand how the bubble could have made a mistake.'

'Perhaps this picture isn't a good likeness, could that be the problem?'

'Maybe, maybe… but I've never come across that problem before, and if Dad had, I'm sure he would have told me about it.'

'You don't think it's dead, do you?'

'Oh flippin' heck, I hope not, I wouldn't want to go back and tell Alex that.'

'No, neither would I.'

Just then, their attention was drawn to a runner in the distance heading in their direction: it was a lady and she had a dog running alongside her.

'Look,' Lucy said, 'maybe we should ask that person, she might have seen Speedy on one of her runs.'

'That's a good idea,' Horla replied, 'let's go over to the path she's on and we'll pop out of the bubble before she turns the corner.'

This they did and, as she approached, she slowed down, seemingly surprised at the sight of a young girl and a dog all alone on the hills; her dog, on the other hand, seemed a little wary at seeing Pip and started barking rather aggressively. The lady then told the dog off and grabbed it by the collar, deciding it would be best to put its lead on for the time being. As she got up close, Lucy produced the photograph and said, 'Excuse me; have you seen this dog on any of your runs?'

To her delight the lady said, 'Yes, I have, in fact not only have I seen it, but I've also been feeding it.'

'*Really?*'

'Yes – does it belong to you?'

'No, it belongs to a boy I know and it has run away and he's heartbroken without it.'

'*Oh,*' the woman said sympathetically, 'I can understand why because it's a lovely dog.'

'Do you know where it is now?' Lucy then asked.

'No I don't, but I've been looking for it. You see, I live on the farm below and a while back it turned up looking very weak and desperately hungry. I tried to entice it closer but it kept on running off and then looking at me from a distance, afraid, I thought, because my dog was about. I then put some food out in the yard, and, after locking my dog in a shed at the back of the farm, watched through a window. It must have been able to smell the food because it came back to the yard and, cautiously, after checking nobody was about, dashed across and ate it as fast as it could. It then ran off, and I thought I would never see it again.'

'And did you?' Lucy asked.

'Well, the following day I saw it watching me from a distance and I felt so sorry for it that I decided to do exactly what I'd done the previous day. I locked my dog up, put out the food and watched. Again it came, ate the food and ran off. This routine continued right up to seven days ago when he ran off and never came back. The reason I'm out running today, as I've done every day since, is in the hope that I might spot the dog, because I'm worried it may have come to some harm. Do you know what its name is?'

'Yes, his name is Speedy.'

'That's quite an appropriate name for a dog so fast.'

'Yes, it is.'

'But such a timid dog; its behaviour was strange,' the lady added sadly, shaking her head – unaware that her own dog was behind her, standing on its back legs, and licking fresh air!

'Well Alex and his mum think he had been a racing dog that was mistreated.'

'Hmm, maybe that's why he was frightened,' the lady said, then asked, 'what's your name?'

'My name's Lucy and this is my grandma's dog, Pip,' Lucy replied.

'Well, my name's Kay, Lucy, and I'll continue to look for Speedy—'

'*Oh, will you?*' Lucy interrupted, 'Alex would be ever so grateful if you find him.'

'Yes I will, and if I do find him I'll let you know and you can tell Alex, I presume that's Speedy's owner?'

'Yes, it is.'

'OK. Now I've a pen and paper here in my bum-bag; we'll exchange phone numbers so we can make contact, how about that?'

'That would be great, Kay, thanks,' Lucy replied.

Lucy then gave both her home phone number and her mum's mobile phone number to Kay, and Kay gave her numbers to Lucy, who promised to ring her if she found Speedy.

Kay then continued on her run, while the girls decided on one more look before they headed for home. This time they decided that, although there was no sign of Speedy, they would get out of the bubble and look anyway; perhaps it knew more than they thought!

23

THE POTHOLE

So back they went to the same spot. As soon as they were on the ground, Pip went on a sniffing mission, the sort of action he took when he was in the park; smelling the routes other dogs had taken. The girls looked at each other – well Horla looked at Lucy and Lucy looked where she thought Horla was – their mouths wide open in surprise.

'Maybe, just maybe, Speedy *has* been here?' Lucy suggested.

'Perhaps, and perhaps he's still here... *but where?*' Horla replied, quizzically.

Lucy decided to use the full length of the lead and let Pip roam where he wanted to. From side to side, then moving forward, he carried on sniffing ahead of them. He seemed to be getting more and

more excited as he went, giving out little barks every now and then.

Then he shot off in the direction of a large clump of ferns, the girls having to run faster to keep up with him. Pip disappeared into the undergrowth and, by the time his companions got there, he couldn't be seen. Lucy shouted him, and just as she did so, she heard a yelp followed by a terrific pull on the lead as it was nearly yanked out of her hand.

She realised Pip had fallen down a hole, how deep it was she didn't know, but she knew she had to get him out. Horla now gave a hand and they both held the lead and gently pulled and pulled: they didn't want to hurt Pip. Eventually he reappeared, looking none the worse for his ordeal, although looking grateful to be back with them, his tail wagging furiously. The girls then went to investigate, crawling in amongst the ferns, but being very careful as they went. After a bit of effort, they discovered the hole, which turned out to be larger than they expected. They wanted to go further inside but thought it better not to. Horla could do lots of things but was sensible enough not to take chances in dangerous situations, just in case she couldn't sort it out: her dad and grandad had taught her that.

Lucy's arms were, by now, covered in scratches and she was just about to ask Horla if she, like her, suspected Speedy could have fallen down there, and could even be dead, when she heard a sound. A skylark was happily singing up above, but, down below, down in what they realised was a deep hole, there was another kind of sound. It was a dog in distress... *it was Speedy!*

What to do now was the next question. They decided to ring Kay, as she was the nearest adult, and they felt sure she would know what to do. She had just got back to the farm as her phone rang, and Lucy, hardly pausing for breath, quickly explained the situation.

'Kay, I think we've, I mean, I've found Speedy,' she said breathlessly. 'He's down a hole over to the left of where I met you on the path.'

Kay seemed as excited as Lucy was, and said, 'OK, stay there, I'll be up in a few minutes with my husband.'

Very shortly they heard the sound of an engine, then, in the distance, fast approaching them was a red quad bike. As it neared, Kay, who was on the back of the bike, gave Lucy a wave. Pip looked relieved that her dog wasn't with her as he didn't like the noisy brute. They found out later his name was Cactus, because of his prickly nature; no wonder Speedy didn't hang around.

As they dismounted, Kay introduced her husband, Ian, who was really keen to see where the hole Lucy had described was. He was a member of a local potholing club and thought he knew every hole in this area, certainly ones big enough to make a dog disappear. Wiping his glasses, he said, 'Now then Lucy, where's this hole you're talking about?'

'It's over here, Ian,' Lucy said, walking towards the ferns, and at the same time stopping Pip, who appeared to understand the question and was tugging on his lead as if to say, *'I found Speedy, not you; I'll show him where he is.'*

Ian came across to Lucy with a powerful torch in his hand, and, on seeing where she was pointing, went to the spot and knelt down. He then lay flat on his stomach and proceeded to crawl into the ferns, knowing that if he walked into them, he could possibly fall into the hole. As the soles of his boots disappeared, his wife, who didn't appreciate how careful he was being, shouted anxiously, 'Please be careful, Ian, we don't want to have to rescue you too.'

'Oh my word,' Ian's voice came back, 'I'm flabbergasted; I've been potholing for thirty years, and here, on my own doorstep, is a pothole I never knew about, in fact nobody knew about... *until now that is,*' he ended triumphantly.

'Never mind your silly pothole,' his wife angrily retorted, 'what about the dog, can you see it?'

Realising he was being told off, Ian recovered from his delight at seeing the pothole, and his attention was immediately drawn to a sad and forlorn sight. Perched on a ledge about three metres down was Speedy, shivering from cold and fear as the light shone on him.

'He's here!' shouted Ian, who had seen Speedy before when the dog was in the farmyard feeding. Fortunately for Speedy, Ian knew exactly what to do next, as he had a lot of experience in this sort of situation. He crawled out backwards, then immediately got on his mobile phone to other members of his club, one of whom was a vet who worked for the RSPCA. As a vital part of the local rescue services, the club had been called out on numerous occasions in the past when animals, and sometimes people, were in distress, and had a set procedure for these situations.

'Don't worry, we'll have him out in no time,' he said to a relieved Lucy.

'Oh thank you so much,' she replied joyfully, 'I can't wait to tell Alex.'

'Well, wait till the vet has had a look at him before you call,' Ian replied. Lucy picked up on his concern realising Speedy could be badly injured and may need to be put to sleep. But she was optimistic and, having completely forgotten the time, was looking forward to seeing Speedy being rescued. It was then that the mobile in her rucksack rang. Looking at her watch before she answered it, she knew she was in trouble.

'Lucy, what on earth's keeping you?' her mum exclaimed. 'Grandma's coming round for tea and she'll be here any minute, I want you home now!'

'Sorry, Mum, but you know I was searching for Speedy, well I've found him, he's stuck down a hole and the rescuers are here trying to get him out.'

'Well that's good news and well done but I need you home now – anyway, exactly where are you?'

Strangely, a lot of static interference came on the line immediately after Lucy's mum asked that question.

'I'm sorry, Mum, you're breaking up. I'll be home right away.'

Lucy, realising that Horla had caused the static, whispered to her forlornly, 'I'd love to see Speedy being rescued but we'd better get back or else I'll be in real trouble.'

'Hmm, I wanted to see him rescued too,' Horla whispered back, while at the same time thinking, *and I think I know how to make that possible.*

Putting the phone back into her rucksack, Lucy said, 'I'm sorry, but I have to go now, Kay.'

'Oh, OK Lucy,' Kay replied, continuing, 'I've got your number so I'll ring and let you know as soon as Speedy is safe.'

'Thank you,' Lucy said, then, rather hastily rushed out of sight before Kay could say any more. She picked up Pip and, on Horla's count of three, jumped up and into the bubble. As the bubble rose into the air, it suddenly occurred to Kay (as Lucy thought it would) that she should offer them a lift, as it was a long way down to the road where, she presumed, Lucy's parents were waiting. She rushed after them, but, to her amazement, the pair where nowhere to be seen. She scratched her head in puzzlement.

My word she's fast, she thought, *either that or she's fallen down another flippin' pothole, and her dog with her.*

24

THE RESCUE

Meanwhile, Horla, Lucy and Pip sped back towards Lucy's house. While doing so, Horla explained what she wanted Lucy to do when she got home, so that they would, if she was correct, see the rescue of Speedy.

'I remember Grandad and Dad talking about this and I reckon I can do it too,' she said confidently.

'Fantastic,' Lucy replied enthusiastically, 'I do so want to see Speedy in real life!'

'I do too, and I'm sure we will; just remember, your rucksack stays outside.'

'OK, got it – rucksack stays outside.'

Not having to take Pip home meant Horla could land the bubble in a secluded part of Lucy's garden where her mum often sunbathed in her bikini.

As soon as it touched down, Lucy and Pip raced to the door where Lucy stopped and removed her rucksack, placing it on the doorstep before going inside as Horla had told her to do.

'Oh, you're back at long last,' said her mum, 'we'll have to start calling you Gulliver; you've had so many travels.'

'Don't be silly, Mum, and besides he was a boy and I'm not,' Lucy laughingly replied. Grandma then came walking out of the kitchen to greet them, when Lucy suddenly said, 'Oh I've forgotten something,' and went back outside.

'Where are you go—' was all Lucy's mum got out of her mouth before she suddenly froze like a statue, and so too did Grandma, who was bending down stroking Pip. He was pleased to see her, although you wouldn't have known it as his tail had stopped wagging – he was frozen like a statue too!

Seeing this, Lucy picked up her rucksack and dashed back to the secluded part of the garden where once more, on Horla's count of three, she jumped up into the bubble, which, with Speedy's picture giving directions, raced off back to the pothole.

***

It was late afternoon and, as they sped on, all sorts of activities were taking place below them: football matches, horse racing, cross country races etc, all coming to an end in the fading light. As they approached the pothole, which had been cleared of all the ferns, the first thing they saw was a green Land Rover, and, they realised, potholing club members who were taking equipment from it. The bubble stopped just above them and the two girls watched and listened as the adults set about their task.

The vet, they soon learned, was called Geoff. He was small and slim but strong, what the adults call "sinewy". He had a helmet on, which had a head torch attached. A rope ladder had been secured and let down into the hole and Geoff was already on it, with just his head peering out. He reached for his bag, which contained all the medicine he might need, and then disappeared completely from view.

It seemed a long time before they heard the crackling noise of the two-way radios and Geoff's voice saying, 'Right, well the situation is that the dog has got a broken leg, so I'm going to give him a sedative then put it in a splint; he's had quite an ordeal but I'm sure he's going to make a full recovery.'

On hearing this, Kay said to Ian, 'That's great news; I'll ring Lucy now and tell her.'

She then put the phone on loudspeaker so Ian could hear Lucy's reaction, knowing she would be so pleased.

'Oh no!' said Lucy on hearing this. 'She's calling me and I'm not there to take her call.'

'Oh yes you are,' replied Horla, giggling as she said it.

'What do you mean? I'm here, not at home and I can't be in two places at once.'

'Shush and listen,' came back the reply.

What happened next made Lucy's jaw drop almost to her toes. Seconds after dialling, she heard Kay speaking to her mum, explaining who she was. She then heard her mum say she would pass the phone over and then, unbelievably, heard her own voice in conversation with Kay. Lucy was dumbfounded. Of all the unusual things she had experienced with Horla over the last few weeks, this, she decided, was the strangest.

'Oh that's really great news, I'll phone Alex and his mum immediately and let them know,' she heard herself saying, thinking as she listened, how grown up she sounded.

Suddenly, the two-way radios sprung into life again and Kay said, 'Hang on, Lucy, Geoff's talking again and I want to hear what he says.'

Lucy and Horla then heard Geoff the vet say, 'Once I get him out, I'll take him home with me, and on Monday I'll take him to the RSPCA centre where I work so that he gets all the attention he needs: the nurses there will make a fuss of him, and, as I said, he'll soon make a full recovery.'

Kay, delighted at the news, restarted the telephone conversation and relayed the information to Lucy for her to pass on to Alex and his mum.

Lucy then heard herself saying, 'Thanks Kay, and please thank Ian and everyone else involved; I'm sure Alex and his mum will ring to thank you too when I tell them all that's happened.'

'I'm sure Ian and everybody else were just happy to help, Lucy, I'm just relieved it's had a happy ending.'

'Yes, so am I, *a very happy ending!'*

Even though she wanted to see Speedy in real life, up in the bubble a confused Lucy's instinct after hearing herself on the phone to Kay was to now rush back home to do the talking.

'Do you think we should be going now Horla?' she asked, a little worried.

'Don't you want to wait until we see Speedy emerge from the hole? That's what we decided on, isn't it?'

'Yes, I do really, but what about me getting back and speaking to Kay.'

'But you did get back, you've just been speaking to her, remember?'

'Oh yes… but… I mean, are you sure your plan will work?'

'It has worked, don't you see, otherwise you wouldn't have spoken to her; now will you please stop worrying, everything will be alright, trust me.'

So Lucy did trust Horla, and they did wait until Speedy emerged from the pothole. This though, took longer than they imagined. The first thing the team had to do was to clear away the remaining ferns, then make the hole slightly larger so they could get Speedy out without hurting him more than he was already, and they had to do it without stones and soil falling into the hole; this was no easy task and took some time.

One of Ian's tasks was to erect a big light on a tripod, as daylight faded and darkness set in, to allow people to continue working. While all this was going on, Kay played a vital role by whizzing down to her farm on the quad bike and collecting flasks of hot soup and coffee to sustain everyone during this arduous task, the bike gaining approval from Horla because of the speed it went.

'Wow, that thing can really shift! I'd love to have a go on it,' she said.

'Now, why am I *not,* surprised,' chuckled Lucy in reply.

Eventually, a harness was lowered down and, very carefully, Speedy was brought to the surface.

He looked a sorry sight. Even in this light they could see he was just a bag of bones, and the nice new bandage on his broken leg made him look even dirtier than he was. However, the girls were sure he was in good hands, and as he was placed gently in the Land Rover by Geoff, who had followed him

out, they decided it was time to depart. As they left, the other members of the team were covering the hole with a strong wooden lid they had constructed and a "DANGER – KEEP OUT" sign was put up. Tomorrow they would come back and put railings up, as they didn't want what happened to Speedy to happen to anyone else.

'Right, let's get home,' said Horla yawning. This set off Lucy yawning and they both smiled. It had been a long day, and for Lucy, without her realising it at that moment, it was going to get even longer.

25

A MOST UNUSUAL
JOURNEY HOME

The bubble slowly rose, then, on reaching a height to clear the tallest hill, it accelerated as it always did when a photograph wasn't involved, right back to where it had started from – in this case Lucy's house. This journey, though, wasn't going to be like the other journeys Lucy had experienced in the bubble – no, nothing like them at all!

The first thing she noticed was that it appeared to be getting lighter. She thought she had been out for so long that it was the next day dawning, because the sun was rising – fast. Then she remembered what she had been taught in school, that the sun comes up in the east and goes down in the west, but she was looking towards the west and the sun was definitely rising in that direction. She looked at her watch to see what time it was and got another shock: the hands were moving and moving pretty quickly – but not clockwise, they were turning anti-clockwise. Lucy gasped as she realised – *they were travelling back in time!*

All around her strange things were happening. The birds were flying once again – but they weren't flying forward, they were flying backwards! The cross country race was still going on; it had obviously just been won as the winner was crossing the finishing line – running backwards, in the direction he had come from, but this time he was last! In the football match, a ball which had crossed the goal line came shooting back out to the goal scorer, then followed him as he dribbled it backwards towards his own

goal! The funniest of all, though, was the horse racing, where the horses and riders were jumping over fences, backwards – with the last horse's tail in the lead!

By the time they reached home it was just as bright as when they had left. As they landed, Lucy immediately ran to the rucksack she'd left behind, picked it up and walked back in the house just as her mum was finishing off her sentence, '—ing to now?'

'Sorry Mum, I left my rucksack on the step, that's all,' she said, carrying on as if nothing had happened.

***

Over tea, Lucy, "The Great Investigator", as her family were jokingly calling her, told them all about how she and Pip had found the missing dog called Speedy. Then she told how they had met Kay who was going to ring once Speedy had been rescued from the hole.

They naturally thought the hole she was talking about was in the hills at the back of their house where lots of local people walked their dogs, and Lucy let them think that. She didn't have to worry that Kay would give the game away as she had already heard the conversation she was going to have with her mum later that evening.

Lucy assured her that Kay would ring and so was allowed to stay up a little later to wait for the call. It was weird when it eventually came. Lucy found herself chuckling inside as she said what she had heard herself say earlier – and chuckling even more because she knew exactly what Kay was going to say in reply.

Lucy ended the call by thanking Kay and telling her she would ring Alex and his mum immediately with the good news. This she did and also gave them the details of the RSPCA centre Speedy was being taken to so they could arrange to pick him up when he was well enough.

As soon as the conversation had ended, a very tired Lucy went upstairs to bed. Soon, she drifted off to sleep, thinking as she did of all the things that had happened that day, and what future adventures with Horla lay ahead. She started to dream, and a smile came on her face as she dreamt of the boy and the talking crisp packet, and of the squadron of geese pooing on the ugly man with the ugly dog. What pleased her most about the day, though, was the fact that she had helped Alex find his dog, and also that he and his mum could now happily move to their brand new house where they would be with their old friends and neighbours – and Speedy! She wouldn't have known that, as she slept, the members of the potholing club were talking about her and had come to a decision.

The following week, the headline in the next town's paper read, *"New pothole found; named, 'Pothole Lucy' after the girl who discovered it!"*

Let's hope her parents never see *that* headline; if they did, they would realise just how far she had travelled, and that would take a *lot* of explaining, wouldn't it?

But then of course, they wouldn't believe her anyway!

Coming soon

The Girl in the Mirror: Isobel's dream... featuring, Lucy and Pip enter a talent competition, The Bull to the Rescue; The Curious Case of the Flying Jockeys, and, The Safari Park incident, where a boy is sprawled on the ground with hungry lions racing towards him, they are five metres away when a mighty roar is heard. The lions stop in their tracks and look around, now afraid that they could get eaten themselves by some mighty creature. And then they saw what had roared, and they started to tremble, too afraid at first to run. Then another almighty roar came forth as the creature came nearer, stalking them like lions stalk their prey. They realised to escape with their lives they needed to make a dash for the bush... for what they were looking at and making them so afraid was Pip: *but it was Pip with a difference!*